# COMEMADRE

# COMEMADRE

Roque Larraquy

*Translated by Heather Cleary*

**COFFEE HOUSE PRESS**

Minneapolis

2018

Coffee House Press books are available to the trade through our primary distributor, Consortium Book Sales & Distribution, cbsd.com or (800) 283-3572. For personal orders, catalogs, or other information, write to info@coffeehousepress.org.

Coffee House Press is a nonprofit literary publishing house. Support from private foundations, corporate giving programs, government programs, and generous individuals helps make the publication of our books possible. We gratefully acknowledge their support in detail in the back of this book.

LIBRARY OF CONGRESS CATALOGING-IN-PUBLICATION DATA
Names: Larraquy, Roque, 1975– author. | Cleary, Heather, translator
Title: Comemadre / Roque Larraquy ; translated by Heather Cleary.
Other titles: Comemadre. English
Description: First English-language edition. | [Minneapolis] :
    Coffee House Press, 2018. | "First published by Editorial Entropía
    as La comemadre, 2010" — ECIP galley.
Identifiers: LCCN 2017056244 | ISBN 9781566895156 (softcover)
Subjects: LCSH: Physicians—Fiction. | Cruelty—Fiction. |
    GSAFD: Dystopian fiction. | Historical fiction.
Classification: LCC PQ7798.422.A76 C6613 2018 | DDC 863/.7—dc23
LC record available at https://lccn.loc.gov/2017056244

Cover images: cross section of human tissue © Komsan Loonprom/ Shutterstock.com; human eye illustration © RYGER/Shutterstock.com; bacteria illustration © Morphart Creation/Shutterstock.com; eye surgery illustration © iStockphoto.com/ilbusca

The advertisement across from the title page was originally published in *Caras y Caretas,* no. 459, July 20, 1907.

PRINTED IN THE UNITED STATES OF AMERICA
25  24  23  22  21  20  19  18        1  2  3  4  5  6  7  8

What predominates in any change is the survival of earlier material. Infidelity to the past is only relative.

—Ferdinand de Saussure,
*Course in General Linguistics*

The middle class will save Argentina.
Its triumph will be felt throughout the world.

—Benjamín Solari Parravicini,
Prophetic psychographic from 1971

# COMEMADRE

| 1907 | *Temperley,*<br>Province of Buenos Aires |
|---|---|

# 1

There are people who don't exist, or who barely do, like Ms. Menéndez. *The head nurse.* She fits entirely into the space of those words. The women who report to her smell and dress alike and call us "Doctor." If a patient takes a turn for the worse due to an oversight or one too many injections, they brim with presence: they exist in errors. Menéndez, on the other hand, never makes a mistake, which is why she's the head nurse.

I watch her whenever I can, trying to find some private gesture, a secret, an imperfection.

I found it. Menéndez's five minutes. She leans against the railing and lights a cigarette. She tends not to look up, so I observe her unnoticed. Her expression suggests an absence of thought, an empty bottle. She smokes for five minutes. In this time she manages to finish only half the cigarette. Her extravagance, her personal indulgence, is putting it out with a dab of saliva on the tip of her finger and tossing it into the trash. She smokes only fresh cigarettes. This is how she enters the world every day, like clockwork, and exists just long enough for me to fall in love with her.

I have many colleagues and still can't tell them all apart. There's a stocky fellow with a mole on his chin who always says hello to me and about whom I remember nothing but his mole. I don't know his name or his specialization. One side of his face sags, and when he speaks—about what, exactly, I couldn't say—he squints as if staring into an intense light.

Each word Sylvia utters is a fly leaving her mouth, and she must avoid speaking to keep their numbers down. I immerse her in freezing water. When I let go she lifts her head, takes a breath, and repeats her question: "You don't see the flies coming out of me?" My not seeing them matters more to her than the cold. I still have no idea why they assigned her to me. I'm not a psychiatrist. I'm confident that the only thing the freezing water does is put her at risk of pneumonia, but the important thing is the persistence of the delusion, which the ice bath should curtail. I promise her a warm bed. All changes must be noted down: if she chooses not to speak, if she asks for her family (she has none, but at least this delusion would be a healthier one), if there are no more flies. She watches them dissolve on the ceiling.

You don't think the thoughts of a nurse. You spend your five minutes smoking a cigarette with a blank expression on your face, as if you were not a woman but merely your woman's work, yet you think about things that are not catheters or serums, things that have no shape.

There she is. A cloud of nurses trails behind her asking for help, advice, medical histories, cleaning products. I'm pomaded. Getting closer. The cloud is easy to disperse. They make way, trying not to invade my personal space. We doctors have earned a bodily right that the nurses, with their enemas and their thermometers, respect in virtually no one else.

"Menéndez!"

"Yes, Doctor Quintana?"

It's lovely to hear her say my name. I give her some instruction or other.

The sanatorium is on the outskirts of Temperley, a few miles from Buenos Aires. It is most active during the day shift, which receives an average of thirty patients. The desolate night shift has been under my charge for the past year. My patients are men who tussle at knifepoint in nearby guesthouses and appreciate our discretion with the law. The nurses are afraid of them. They file out along the path that cuts through the park before nightfall. I don't recall ever seeing Menéndez leave. She's always here. Does she live in the sanatorium? I make a note: Ask.

Night arrives and there is nothing to do. Might as well walk the halls looking for a conversation or a game of cards to give the time some shape. A nurse leans against the wall with her hands in her pockets. Her associate stares at the floor.

Doctor Papini trots toward me with his index finger to his lips in an appeal for silence. He has freckles and a habit of fondling the breasts of unconscious old ladies. He occasionally confides the details of his life to me, and I find his deliberate obscenity vaguely repulsive. He guides me to a small room.

"Do you know what's in the morgue right now, Quintana?"

"The red wine you hid there on Tuesday."

"No, that's all gone. We had to give a few bottles to the cleaning lady to keep her quiet. Come with me."

Papini opens a drawer and takes out an anthropometric instrument he bought on the Paseo de Julio and was never allowed to use in the sanatorium, on Ledesma's orders. He is sweating, exophthalmic, and smells like lemon. This indicates that he is happy, or believes that he is happy. His personality is defined by this sort of thing.

"Strange things are happening, Quintana. Women are locking themselves in the washroom and spending long stretches of time on the bidet. They say nothing when they come out.

This ritual isn't about hygiene or masturbation, I assure you. I myself opened my wife's legs and smelled her: nothing. She told me she'd been brushing her teeth. But I heard her in there! There's no confusing the sound of a bidet. I'm incapable of many things, my friend, especially of killing my wife. But there are those who could, you see. Who would make her confess, because this ritual of water and ceramic is a threat to all men. Women use cosmetics to erase their features, squeeze themselves into corsets, and have many orgasms, yes? A number that would dry us out completely. They're different. They come from a special kind of ape that was previously an otter, and before that was a bluish amphibian or something with gills. Their heads are a different shape, too. They shut themselves in with the bidet to think moist thoughts that suit the contours of their heads. The threat. I'm a good man, I don't have the stomach to do anything about it. But there are those who do. They grab them by the hair and demand to know why they spend so much time on the bidet, and if the women don't answer, they carve them up with their knives. These men are as different from us as women are. They came from a different ape than we did: an inferior species, but robust and enduring. There's one in the morgue. We're going to take his measurements. You'll see that his cranium matches the description of atavism, of a born killer. We have to do it now because they're taking him away in the morning. You're an intelligent man, but stubborn. I'm going to bury you in evidence."

"This fellow killed his wife because she wouldn't tell him what she was doing on the bidet?"

"It's a metaphor, Quintana."

As we step into the hall I remember that there are no bidets in the sanatorium bathrooms. Menéndez can hide nothing from me. No moist thoughts, no threats. Papini's speech accelerates as he walks toward the morgue, leaving a trail of lemon in his wake.

"It's the so-called qualitative leap, Quintana. At night we come up with daring plans that would change us completely, were they to become a reality. But these plans dissolve in the morning light, and we go back to being the same mediocrities as before, doggedly ruining our own lives. This doesn't happen to you? With these men, it's different. Why do you think they're still around, if they're so inferior to us? It's a question of adaptation: they *act*. They carry out the plans they make at night. What's more, they're depraved. They wear too much pomade, smell like tobacco, sweat bile, and masturbate frequently. They have no morals. They do, however, have an ethics that neither you nor I could comprehend, which involves eradicating us. Do you understand?"

"How do you know they wear too much pomade?"

"You're taking me very literally, Quintana."

We enter the morgue, the brightest room in the sanatorium. With his freckles, Papini looks like a bedraggled adolescent. If the men he just described to me do exist, he is one of them. The body is on the table. Menéndez must never see me under this light.

"He was hanged by his cellmates. Do you see the look in his eyes, their color? There's the line of bruising at the neck. Look at his forehead, how narrow it is. Asymmetrical cranium, smaller than average for a Caucasian, convex in the right temporoparietal zone. Ideas must have come to him all squashed. How much energy would it take to move that jaw? Compare and contrast, Quintana. You aren't what anyone would call handsome, but your features are in the right place. Your balls, well, I don't know. You tell me, right? A man's balls are his own business. But just look at him: left eye three or four millimeters below the right; huge ears; lower canines more prominent than the upper. This man didn't chew, he shredded meat. Lift his foot, Quintana, bend his leg at the knee. See that? Prehensile. A man with a small head, to keep things simple, and teeth made for crushing our femurs in a single bite, covered in hair. Do you see? A few years from now, we'll be able to identify these animals fresh out of their mothers. We can empty their nuts if they're male, or take out their uterus if they're female."

"Why not just kill them outright?"

"You're not taking me seriously, Quintana."

"I hate to be rude, Papini. But this man is an isolated case."

"We'll measure you and your thick skull, then. Or someone else, for a point of comparison."

"Let's measure Ms. Menéndez."

She steps into my office, accompanied by Papini. She knows this meeting falls outside her job description. It shows in her face, which is not her own, and in the backward slant of her body.

The explanations we give are few and vague. She realizes her head is at stake but does not know that Papini is hoping to find a criminal (or not, either result would be valid) and I am hoping for a wife. She takes a seat and allows herself to be measured. She has pale skin, blue eyes, and a slightly crooked nose. Her response to pain (Papini is pricking her finger) is modest.

I don't dare speak to her. What primate lurks beneath the surface of Ms. Menéndez? None, I think. I might assign her an amphibian lineage, but nothing more.

I look out the window. A line of ants emerges from a crack in the wall and inscribes a large circle as it advances. The front of the line forms the circumference, and the others fill it in until the crack and the ants disappear and all that is left on the wall is a brittle, chitinous blotch of legs. I assume their worldview is defined by this circularity.

I find Sylvia sitting on the edge of her bed. She asks me to open the window and inquires about the weather. It's cold. The news pleases her: flies can't stand the cold. She is still talking about flies. I think, in parentheses, about Menéndez. The two curved lines bend toward each other, trapping Menéndez inside my head and my head inside the parentheses . . .

Should I allow myself these intrusions, these fantasies? Is this healthy? I don't even know her first name. Why am I blushing? Have I no shame?

I need to switch primates. Carry out in the day the plans I make at night.

"Have you ever been in love, Sylvia?"

She is saying something about bundling up in flies but goes along with the change of topic.

"Yes."

"With whom?"

"I'd prefer not to say, Doctor."

"Was it mutual?"

"Yes."

"And how did this man tell you he loved you?"

"He said, 'Sylvia, I think of you often.'"

"He lied."

Where is she? It has to be now. Before I don't know what to say. Not that I know now, either, but the initiative is there.

The doctor with the mole says that Menéndez is in the sanatorium, but he doesn't know where, and it would be best not to disturb her if she's in her room.

How can she live in a sanatorium?

I watch her walk into Ledesma's office and am drawn toward her like a magnet, only to have some insolent creature, or perhaps it was her, slam the door in my face.

I'm reminded that there's a special meeting in progress. We crowd around Ledesma's door. I have to wait my turn, same as the others. The human heap of my colleagues. Doctor Gigena is an enthusiast: he wears glasses, and it's said that the patients like him best because he distracts them with jokes during their injections. According to Doctors Gurian and Sisman, Gigena's penchant for acting like a funny uncle undermines his professional stature. Papini cracks wise on the subject.

More doctors arrive. Our bellies begin to graze, our buttons catch, static electricity stands our whiskers erect. We would have gone on like that, surreptitious pawings punctuating the wait, but Mr. Allomby, on whom our salaries depend, appears, and we clamor to attention. He almost never visits the sanatorium. The meeting is more important than we'd thought. Time to dig the skeletons out of our closets and make a gallows of them.

Someone greets him in English, with terrible pronunciation. Afraid of sullying his aura, we suck in and pile up even more tightly. This time, however, we are not synchronized in our efforts. One straggler trips over the feet of another and crashes into the office door. It swings open.

We see Ledesma on all fours under his desk. Some of us find getting on all fours in a train station objectionable, but we see nothing wrong with an upstanding fellow doing so in the privacy of his own office. There are others, however, who consider assigning him a nickname, refusing to follow his orders, and demanding his resignation for impropriety. This difference of opinion makes us uncomfortable. We hold our breath until Ledesma feels our eyes on him. He turns to look at us.

"Not yet . . . No hora," says Mr. Allomby, closing the door.

Ledesma and Mr. Allomby are seated at the desk. The meekest huddle close to this nucleus of authority, leaning forward in search of approval and protection. The more self-assured among us sit further away, cool and collected, bellies self-satisfied.

"Were you able to catch it, Menéndez?" Ledesma shouts.

Menéndez steps into the office, a squawking duck in her hands. It's quite an entrance. The eyes of several of my colleagues fall on her for the first time and remain. She exists by order of the director.

"Put it on that table," says Ledesma.

The glass tabletop is too slippery for the duck. When it regains its balance, it returns to the impassivity characteristic of its species. Next to it is a wooden box of average size. Its lid, which opens down the middle, has a large, round aperture at its center, bordered by the word *ergo*. Under the lid is a blade that shoots out horizontally with the speed and force of a crossbow. On the sides of the box, next to reliefs of Louis XVI and Marie Antoinette, are the words *cogito* and *sum*, respectively. The phrase and figures clearly bear allegorical weight, which diminishes the charm of the whole.

"Our poor Cartesian duck," quips Ledesma.

He slides the duck into the guillotine through a trapdoor underneath and sticks its head through the opening. Then, just like that, he activates the device. The blade moves so quickly that not a drop of blood is spilled. The Cartesian duck's head remains on the *ergo*. It seems to have felt nothing. It looks at us. Or thinks the thoughts of a duck. It stays like that for a few seconds, honking occasionally, before its eyes and its foray into this world come to a close.

I can't tell if Menéndez is watching or if she chose to look away. In any event, she's the one who has to remove the body, which she wraps in a clean cloth before taking her leave of us.

"Medium-rare, please," says Ledesma.

We wait for an explanation.

"Take this as an example," says Ledesma.

"What are you trying to tell us? That birds of a feather flock together? That there will be cuts to the staff? That heads will roll?"

"No, Papini," replies Ledesma. "The reason for this preamble, which I hope has struck you as singular, even visionary, is right here in these papers I am about to read."

*Before the guillotine, capital punishment was a public spectacle with an established cast: the executioner, the condemned, and the rabble. The show, which was both cathartic and didactic, was no less effective for the predictability of its denouement.*

*With the invention of the guillotine, capital punishment becomes a technical matter. The figure of the executioner is reduced to the meager role of machinist. The austere practicality of this new method leaves no room for style.*

*The executioners, however, refuse to give up their characteristic gesture of lifting the head of the condemned for the rabble to see, once the task has been carried out.*

*a) The executioner offers decisive proof of his performance, not as a matter of personal pride, but as a means of gaining recognition and reward.*

b)  *The rabble adores simple, categorical statements. The head serves as a period at the end of a sentence. Everyone is happy. The executioner as aphorist.*

*(a) and (b) seem to exhaust all possible explanations for the act. But the executioner knows the alphabet of death from beginning to end. Starting with (c), there are more personal reasons, which represent favors or concessions afforded the condemned. This is the executioner's secret rebellion.*

*It is a little-known fact among those outside the profession that the head remains conscious with full use of its faculties for nine seconds after being severed from the torso. Lifting the head, the executioner gives his victim one last, waning glimpse of the world. As such, he not only contravenes the very idea of punishment, he also turns the crowd into the spectacle.*

*For the decapitated individual to remain lucid, certain rules must be observed:*

a)  *He or she must be awake at the moment of decapitation. Observance of rule (a) is directly proportional to the individual's courage.*

b)  *He or she must face the blade; that is, he or she must face the heavens. This is not a metaphor for recovering one's faith, but rather a practical consideration. Individuals who receive the blow on the backs of their necks are rendered unconscious by the impact.*

c)  *Placement of the cleft. For men, below the Adam's apple. For women, above the line of the rosary. Avoid cutting at an angle.*

d)  *A boisterous crowd is preferred, to stimulate the decapitated individual.*

*Executioners instill this knowledge in their sons, along with more ethereal rules (if the individual is a woman, direct her gaze away from the masses), as training for the task they will*

*one day perform. The secret unites them in affectionate com-*
*plicity and is passed from generation to generation like the black*
*habit.*

The duck and the reading leave us speechless. Ledesma explains
that the text is from a study conducted in France by an emi-
nent coroner, translated into Spanish from an English version
that Mr. Allomby himself rendered from the French original. Menéndez hands us each a typewritten copy with our
surname printed in the margin. Mine is misspelled: Qintana,
without the *u*.

"I'll confess that at first," Ledesma continues, "I read this
document grudgingly. Mr. Allomby shared it with me because
he wanted to know whether its hypothesis could be scientifically corroborated."

"What hypothesis?" Gurian asks. "The nine seconds
of consciousness? What the severed head observes? What
hypothesis?"

"The first is perfectly easy to prove—just look at our duck.
I was obviously referring to the second. To put it plainly,
Mr. Allomby asked a favor of me and I couldn't say no, no
matter how skeptical I might have been. I spent a whole year
working on it and discovered, to my pleasant surprise, that
the hypothesis can indeed be proven."

Some sycophant asks how.

"First, I would like you all to share your misgivings. From
left to right, please."

"There are no facts here, no references. On what does this
Frenchman base his claims?" asks Gigena.

"The doctor is an authority on forensic science in Europe."

"Good for him," Gigena retorts.

"And study guillotine," Mr. Allomby offers in his broken Spanish.

"Patriotically," adds Ledesma.

Menéndez returns during this brief silence.

"I'd like to draw your attention, dear colleagues," Gurian begins, "to several stumbling blocks in this so-called document. I don't doubt the good intentions of the director, who has so magnanimously shared it with us and solicited our opinions. But this is no more than the oral history of executioners presented as an irrefutable truth. I wonder: the hypothetical first executioner, the one who discovered this business of the nine seconds—how did he know?"

"Simple," replies Ledesma. "He is a keen observer. He recognizes that the gaze is not empty, that the eyes can see. A second executioner, no less perceptive, notices that the heads make faces of pleasure or discontent."

"Don't forget, Director, that most executioners were illiterate and, as a result, could not grasp abstract realities."

"This seems like an abstraction to you because you're a man of culture, Gurian. We should be talking about intuition."

"I'll cede the floor to one of my less-cultured colleagues, then," Gurian replies.

Next up is Papini, who doesn't demand an apology because he is citric and happy: we aren't here to discuss his trespasses. His skeletons skitter back into the closet.

"In theory, I'll sign on for any experiment the director proposes. Since we're talking about heads, however, it seems reasonable to mention that a phrenological study could be of great interest."

"You know what I think about all that," Ledesma says, "but I'm willing to consider it. The experiment I'm proposing must be broad in scope. What's your opinion, Sisman?"

"I don't agree," Sisman answers, leaning back.

"Explain," hisses Mr. Allomby.

"We don't know what kind of experiment the director is proposing," Sisman replies.

"Let us suppose," says Ledesma, "that what this document claims is true. If we could corroborate it scientifically, we'd be answering a great many questions. We'd be exploring territory that has, until now, belonged exclusively to religion: what is death, and what comes after death?"

"So your foundational premise is that something comes after death," I say, raising my voice. "That doesn't seem very rigorous to me."

"I have no foundational premise," Ledesma replies.

"Well, that doesn't seem very scientific, either."

"Your notion of scientific inquiry is quite conservative, Quintana."

"And your proposal is the stuff of cheap novels, Ledesma."

"You have no idea what I'm proposing."

That will suffice. I conclude my rhetorical acrobatics, which were for Menéndez's benefit, anyway, and cede the floor to the director. He is not angry with me because I made sure to smile toothily at him throughout the confrontation.

"This is what I propose: we select a group of terminally ill patients and sever their heads without damaging their vocal apparatus, using a technique I developed on palmipeds. I'll explain that part later. We then ask the heads to tell us what they observe. Mr. Allomby will pay us handsomely for our efforts."

It is exhausting to be a man of great convictions. Minor ones, however, are within easy reach. *It's better to be an upstanding member of the middle class than a wealthy crook,* or *One drink too many could ruin a young lady's life.* Things get simpler with time.

Another night, another set menu. We've already discussed the money. We've arranged the details of how we'll be paid. What did we do before today, without that money in our future? Wait for our next patient?

We lift our knives, cut the grilled meat, and raise it to our mouths. We were talkative when dinner began, but now the silence is absolute. We chew. This is how I want to remember us: in a celebratory mood. Mr. Allomby eats his asado with the table manners of someone taking afternoon tea. He is intent on looking English. Menéndez sits at the other end of the table. Eating a salad. She is withdrawn, but no one seems to care; there are more immediate pleasures. I want more wine. Want her to see me sweat.

Doctor Gurian sticks his fingers in his mouth, removes his dentures, and starts talking with them. The dentures are quite garrulous and end up leading the conversation. They speak of bovine sinews caught in their darkest depths and nibbles delivered to women's rear ends.

Mr. Allomby serves himself more wine. He says, in his Spanish, that Argentina's extermination of the natives guaranteed better teeth for future generations. Strengthened molars and national unity. Vanquished underarm odor. Fueled the straight razor industry. (He informs us, as a curiosity, that Indians don't grow beards—as if we didn't know that already.) Safeguarded the hymens of our nieces and daughters. Improved the quality of our brothels.

Ledesma skewers a piece of meat and swings it around as he talks, splattering us with its juices. He says he went to Berlin once, and witnessed a fire in a cabaret.

Our thoughts turn to German women.

It started with a cigarette. The fire spread, and everyone was trapped inside. When it reached the liquor, the whole place went up. No one was saved. The only thing to do was wait for the blaze to burn itself out. Ledesma spent the night discussing the fire with other onlookers. It was morning before he realized that, as a doctor, he might be of use in the collection of bodies.

Papini interrupts to say that his mother's coffin contains only a leg. We waste a moment imagining what it must be like to bring flowers to a leg. No one asks what happened to the rest of his mother.

Ledesma seizes the opportunity to take a bite of his meat, straight from the skewer. He says he helped the fire brigade lift blackened slabs and sift through the rubble. He found three charred chorus girls; one of them was carrying a mother-of-pearl cigarette case in her pocket. He still has it.

Gigena rests his hand on the hot grill. Then he shows us his palm, crossed by three perfect red lines. He says the human body is not prone to catching fire at random: intense heat can be administered, its limits tested.

Mr. Allomby points his fork at you, Menéndez. And says to me quietly:

"That woman. I love."

*Caras y Caretas Magazine*
Buenos Aires, July 20, 1907

*Temperley Sanatorium. A unique facility for the treatment of Cancer and Blood Disorders.*

*The cancer serum developed by Professor Beard of the University of Edinburgh (England) has been shown to cure the disease completely. The serum has been administered in major hospitals across Europe and the United States, and in Temperley Sanatorium, with surprising results.*

*Temperley Sanatorium is the only facility in the Republic of Argentina authorized by Doctor Beard to provide this treatment.*

*Free consultations are held between 10 a.m. and 12 p.m. at Temperley Sanatorium, Temperley Station. In Buenos Aires, further details are available at 332 Calle Bolívar from 1 to 3 p.m.*

## 2

Mr. Allomby will try to dazzle you with his red hair and his status. I hope you are the woman I hope you are. When he walks up to you and talks through his teeth at you, I want you to lift your chin as if to say, "What?" like he'd just asked you to manage a brothel. I trust you will.

Could my sense of urgency be robbing me of my style? I'd like to think you want a man with style.

A specious advertisement is published in one of the country's most popular magazines. Well-heeled men and women read it at home. They leave it on their nightstands. A week later, it becomes property of the housemaids. A housemaid's world-view is always about a week behind the times. They read the advertisement and know it's selling a lie, but their notion of hope is less abstract than that of their employers. They mention it to a family member with cancer. The diseased individual travels to Temperley Sanatorium and asks for the cancer serum developed by Dr. Beard of the University of Edinburgh, in England. Edinburgh, however, is in Scotland: Mr. Allomby inserted this error to ward off knowledgeable or detail-oriented persons. Ledesma says that working with uneducated subjects will keep the accounts of death from being tainted by the inanities of polite speech. Those are his exact words.

The terminally ill look at us as though we had our backs to them. Some say, very quietly, *I'll do whatever you ask.*

For the very first time, the sanatorium's halls are crowded. We make our rounds reviewing papers, avoiding eye contact.

We discuss clinical histories loudly, using neologisms and improvised Latin terminology. People step aside, make themselves small. Every bed is occupied. Every vein tapped. The innocuous serum drips, liberating.

The objective for this first stage is to get them to trust the sanatorium's staff. In the second stage, the treatment will begin to "fail" and their hopes will crumble one by one. The patient will be told that he or she is one of the few (12 percent of all cases) for whom the serum does not achieve the desired result. We will reappear, imbued with authority, to suggest that they do something useful with their deaths: donate themselves to science. But it's not time to propose this just yet. Their heads remain in place.

Sylvia is waiting for me next to the tub, swirling the ice with her fingers. Over time, she's gotten used to the cold. But that's not how this works. Immersion therapy is required only for crises or true delusions. She must not be allowed to grow comfortable with insanity, or ice.
"Are you thinking about him?"
"About who, Doctor?"
"That man. The one who said he loved you."
"There's no need."
"You've forgotten him already?"
"Why would I?"
"No ice today. Put on a robe, we're going for a stroll around the grounds."

The novelty of taking a walk makes her aware that she is under treatment. She hasn't left her room in four months. She insists that I not lead her by the arm.

Cancer fills the hallway with first and last names. New faces that demand her undivided attention. She greets them all with the meticulous courtesy often seen in the mentally ill. When she steps through the front door, she is blinded by the sun. Now I do take her arm. She needs to pick up the pace.

"Tell me a little about this man. How did he tell you he was interested in you?"

"I was the one who said it. He wanted it that way."

"What you did was rather undignified, Sylvia."

"What would you have done in my place, Doctor?"

"You're talking too much. Can't you see you're covered in flies?"

She nods. Her face is buzzing. She falls silent, wide-eyed. She leans her head back. A hand tilts it forward again.

"What do you want, Papini?"

"Hello."

He is holding his measuring instrument in his other hand. He opens it and fits it around Sylvia's head. She does not resist. Caucasian, symmetrical features, negligible superciliary arch. She does not fit the description of atavism.

"Do you use the bidet when you go to the bathroom?" he asks.

"No," she replies.

Papini looks at me knowingly.

I make my way down a crowded staircase, accidentally stepping on a patient's foot. He apologizes. Why can't they line up on the veranda?

"It's too cold out, Doctor," says one of the nurses.

As I reach the next step, the same nurse announces that something is on fire.

We don't know what it is yet. We assume it's not inside the sanatorium because there's no screaming or running. We step out onto the grounds: it's the groundskeeper's shed. He stands a few yards away, observing the scene with the rest of us.

It's not what anyone would call a raging inferno, but it coats the wood like an aura. It's quite lovely. The nearest tree gives off a pleasant smell of burnt leaves. That's pretty much it. I turn and head for the empty reception area. I see Menéndez looking over paperwork. Her back is to me.

I stand so my feet are aligned with hers. Must I approach her now, or do I have some time to spare? Time it is. One of my shoelaces extends across the room, laces itself through her shoe, inches up her uniform, wraps itself around each of her buttons, and ties itself in a delicate bow at her neck. If I gave a good kick, those buttons would go flying.

"I need to talk to you, Menéndez."

"Yes?"

"Over coffee, if you don't mind."

"Come again?"

"Coffee."

"You want me to bring you a coffee?"

"No, I was saying that . . ."

"I can't hear you from over there, Doctor. Could you step in a bit? I don't want my uniform smelling of smoke."

I walk over and stand in front of her.

"To talk over you, Menéndez, if you don't mind. A coffee."

"Excuse me?"

"I want you to have a coffee with me. Talk."

"About something in particular?"

"It would be a good chance . . . You know. The day-to-day can be so . . . We barely know each other, am I right?"

"I can't this week, Doctor. Maybe next."

I love her madly. I want to stumble and fall into her so she can feel the raging erection tearing at my pants. Mr. Allomby walks in. He asks where everyone is, why the groundskeeper's shed is on fire, and if anyone is handling it. Menéndez starts giving him the three answers.

I look out the window: there are the ants, marching around their crack in a perfect circle. They are the animal reality nearest to me (I could go down there and smudge out that circle with my foot), along with the flies in Sylvia's face, Papini's apes, the Cartesian duck, and the hypothetical amphibian lurking inside Menéndez.

Every so often, Ledesma turns in his chair and launches himself at his little allegorical guillotine, activating it over and over as he listens to me. I've just told him that I think it might be necessary to "review the—for lack of a better term—*ethical* aspect of the experiment, in the hope that . . ." and I feel an urgent need to erase my mouth, grab a scalpel and cut myself a new one, and then start over.

"Would you like a coffee?" he interrupts me to ask.

"No, thank you."

"You're an honorable man, Quintana. The experiment concerns you, turns your stomach, and you've come here to tell me. Right to my face."

I understand now. A year of work down the drain. No more Menéndez, no more *Hello, Doctor,* no more salary. Now I move to some little backwater. *Hey, Doc.* A house with a yard, bachelorhood, a chicken coop, manure, a wood-burning stove.

"Your colleagues, Quintana . . . Your colleagues . . . None of them came to discuss this with me. They must be wearing out their rosaries right now, wondering whether they're going to hell or what. You're different. Trustworthy."

"Thank you."

"This business of speculating with the lives of cancer cases is pretty distasteful, wouldn't you say? I agree. You need mettle, yes, but you can't rub out the basic emotions that make us men, make us human. When we cut off that first head, that's when we'll see who's who. The one with the steady hand, the one who feels no pity for the patient, that's who we'll need to fire. Because God only knows what he's capable of."

"Are you talking about someone in particular?"

"I'm saying I agree with you. Now, tell me something."

"What?"

"Tell me you don't think it's shameless to ask the patient to waste the final seconds of this life telling us what he's glimpsed on the other side. Honestly, it's disgusting. Coffee!" he shouts over his shoulder, then returns to his earlier tone. "You're sure you don't want any?"

"No, thank you."

"You're expecting me to say that science should always come first, or that redemption lies hidden in the experiment. But I won't. You know why? Because redemption doesn't exist, at least, not in the sense of moral serenity. The goal is to discover what comes with death? Great. That's what we'll do, because we have the means, and because we were the first to think of it. If the results help men be better men, well, great."

A nurse walks in with coffee. Ledesma smiles at her. He settles back into his chair and interlaces his fingers, looking at me without any ulterior motive.

"If you want in, Quintana, fantastic. If you'd rather take a step back, that's fine, too. You're a true professional. Would you like to talk about something else?"

"For the moment . . ."

"Good, good." He pats my hand. "Did I ever tell you about my grandparents? Lovely people. Older folk, passed, of course. They had a big house surrounded by country-side and Argentine things. I spent my summers with them. You might say, how boring for a child. Not at all. There were guinea pigs and a collection of porcelain figurines I wasn't allowed to touch. I mention this because I broke one. Scared of being punished, I hid in the forest for a whole day, but the cold got to me. I felt feverish and had to go back. My grandmother slapped me—only once, but what a slap it was—and sent for the doctor. The help laid me down in my grandparents' enormous bed and covered me with a sheet, a blanket, a comforter, and the embroidered shawl that gave the bed a feminine touch. Under there, I could smell the concentrated scent of my grandparents. Of old bodies. The fever went away, but that smell stayed with me a good long while, until I was twelve or thirteen and ejaculated for the first time. What a feeling, am I right? Do you remember? I was astonished. I brought my hand close to my face and looked at my semen. I smelled it, and do you know what I realized, Quintana? It was the same odor that had saturated that bed."

He pauses. Mr. Allomby is walking into his office wearing an outrageous hat. He greets us. We have to stand.

"Well, well. Look who we have here!" Ledesma jubilates. "How are you?"

"Machine is ready," says Mr. Allomby, looking at me. "Are you . . . me go?"

"He's asking you to have a look at the device with him," Ledesma says. "We'd like your opinion, Quintana."

"Thank you," says Mr. Allomby.

"And what about your grandparents?"

"Perhaps the moral of the story is . . . it's about being honorable, I suppose. I'd have to think about it. Because they were honorable people, Quintana, despite the smell."

The device is a polished mahogany box. Its lid opens down the middle and has a large, round aperture at its center. The person enters through a door at the side and sits down, and the two halves of the lid fit perfectly around his or her neck. Mr. Allomby, who sits inside pretending to be a person, says he can breathe without difficulty.

He steps out of the box, opens the lid, and shows me its inner workings. There is a sharp blade that shoots out horizontally with the speed and force of a crossbow. There is a ventilation system to make the vocal cords vibrate when the head is called upon to speak. There is a trapdoor at the bottom for dropping the body into a storage room in the basement. Mr. Allomby stresses the precision of the design: the cut and drop will take half a second, and the ventilation, synchronized with the head, will run for nine. What am I doing here? Does he want my opinion?

No. He wants to talk about Menéndez. In fact, he's already launched in, and I'm left asking myself how he changed the subject so quickly.

"You know my truth, Mr. Quintana."

"Doctor," I say. "What truth?"

"That I love her."

"Don't worry. I won't tell a soul."

"I want your help me with her."

"You have my word. But don't start acting all Argentine and go rushing in."

He shows me his hands. His palms are sweaty.

"See? I'm so nervous when I talk on Menéndez. You . . ."
I take his hands and pull out my handkerchief.
"Here," I interrupt him. "Allow me."

I'll say things you never expected to hear. Sweet words. Hard words sometimes, too, so you'll know who wears the pants. And you'll be the one who takes mine off, like you do with the patients. On the clock and off. We'll go out to dinner once a week. And to the opera. When no one's around, I'll nibble your backside. I'll give you a stole to cover your neck, and you'll remove it only for me.

The door says *Office of the Head Nurse.* I knock, and it swings open. It's dark inside. Could she be asleep?

Don't go in. Go in, saying, *Excuse me.* Stick my head in. Go in, turn on the light, and stay near the door, just in case.

False options. The real question is whether to make a restrained entrance or a virile one. Staying out here means failure. A restrained entrance builds trust. The virile entrance is more daring. Do I want to build trust?

I need to switch primates. Be a virile Quintana. A charging Quintana.

I open the door and turn on the light, vocalizing a "Menéndez" that ricochets off every wall. She's not here. No one is. I can stay for a moment to gather information. Examine her belongings without touching them. Maybe touch them just a little.

I see a portrait of President Figueroa Alcorta hanging above her dresser, a glass bottle of perfume, never used, and a pack of inexpensive cigarettes.

I shouldn't be here. I feel like a swine. What if I peeked in her closet?

Don't think, just open the door and close it quickly. Take in as much as you can and don't linger, because that's how you get caught. Luckily, the door doesn't make any noise. The closet contains two uniforms, numerous boxes, an evening gown, which is unexpected, and something furry all the way in the back that looks like a muff, but I can't quite make it out because I'm already shutting the door.

I process the information. The uniforms represent her professional dedication, the closed boxes are her secrets, the evening gown is her willingness. There's no time for more sophisticated interpretations, so I settle for those, for now. I set aside all questions about the furry thing in the back. No pun intended: that muff could be my undoing.

I catch the scent of cigarette smoke coming from behind me. I turn with an accusatory little hop, expecting to see the version of Menéndez's face I least want to see, her expression of utter disdain. But no. The smoke is coming from a door off to the side. The one that leads to the bathroom, which is ajar.

She heard me. She saw me going through her things. She's smoking in there, shut in the bathroom for her five minutes, because she knows I spy on her. In her smoky discretion, she seems to be saying, "You can still leave. We can pretend this never happened."

My first instinct is to do as she says. My feet turn toward the door like a pair of rats, but the rest of my body is still paralyzed by shock. I'm caught in a moment of indecision I wouldn't wish on anyone.

There will be no forgiveness if I sneak out now, confirming her opinion of me. A virile Quintana, a charging Quintana. I open the bathroom door. Love will absolve me.

Inside, Papini sits on the toilet, smoking and looking despondently at the water burbling up from the only bidet in the sanatorium. Menéndez's bidet. Droplets have splashed onto his shoes.

"It's you," he says.

"What are you doing here, Papini?"

"I'm in love with Menéndez."

I look down at my hand, make a fist, and punch him in the jaw. I grab him by the throat, throw him over the tub, and kick him in the balls. He spits blood and a tooth. Aside from the odd skirmish in grade school, I've never been in a fight. It feels fine, but its effect is short-lived, and I've already calmed down. I'll lose interest if it goes on much longer.

His eyes squeezed shut by the pain, Papini feels around for the cigarette that fell beside him, brings it to his lips, and takes a pull. A red stain spreads across the paper. He starts to cry.

He cries harder, choking, coughing. I look for a towel to dry him off and plug his mouth, but there aren't any. There must be towels in the closet. Because of some strange acoustic phenomenon, Papini's wailing is louder out here than inside the bathroom, and it's probably even louder in the hallway, like he's howling into a funnel. I swing the closet door open.

Menéndez and two of the nurses are watching me from the hall.

"Help me with this, would you?" I say, raising my voice. "Doctor Papini's broken his face."

Which will you be? Head Nurse or Menéndez? Will you attend to his injuries or get angry because there's no excuse for going through a woman's closet?

"Take care of Doctor Papini," she instructs the nurses, who are there so she won't have to decide right away.

The girls run toward the bathroom.

Menéndez sits on the edge of her bed and stares at the profaned closet.

"What would you do in my place?" she asks.

"I wouldn't jump to any conclusions. I'm happy to explain everything, if you'll allow me to, over a cup of coffee."

"I'm not jumping to any conclusions."

"I appreciate that, Menéndez."

"But I'm not having a coffee with you, either."

This is my inner primate. How many of these backdoor Brunos will I have to pummel, mutilate, destroy? I push the gurney carrying Papini and the new gap in his teeth, through which he smiles up at me (smiles!) because, without even trying to, he's taken me out of the running, knocked me down a peg, hung me out to dry, stolen my golden goose, stripped me of my decorum.

*530 intakes registered between August 1 and October 1. A solution of water, glucose, and vanilla extract labeled "Dr. Beard's Serum" administered orally to 498 cancer patients in two daily doses, eight hours apart, in addition to injections of morphine at the physician's discretion, not declared to the patients or their relatives. 32 patients not admitted for treatment due to imminent demise. 133 patients with tumorous growths in the pancreas, 109 in the kidneys, 94 in the liver, 60 in the stomach, 35 in the ovaries, 32 in the lungs, 22 in the prostate, 12 in the gallbladder, 1 on the palate. The stated interval produces 43 deaths, 18 suspensions of treatment, and 2 cases cured by divine grace, presented to the patients as evidence of the efficacy of Dr. Beard's Serum.*

A nurse has just handed us the report. Papini keeps his distance but says something funny to Sisman about cap-toe shoes, and I'm the only one wearing a pair.

The patients don't take their eyes off us. We're about to have a meeting, yes? To discuss what to do with you all. Not as coldly as you assume, but we're not exactly giving ourselves heartburn over it, either.

The office door opens. There's a duck on the table. Another decapitation? Ledesma confides to me in a whisper that today's duck is symbolic. I take my place in an overstuffed chair near him and Mr. Allomby. A few of my colleagues grumble in their uncomfortable seats, at odds with their buttocks, thinking I landed a good spot because I pushed others out of the way. Others can tell I've gotten cozy with the administration and don't know whether to hate me or what.

The last to sit are Gigena and Gurian, who shoot conspiratorial glances at me. My complicity with them is more scrupulous: I do not return their gaze.

Menéndez closes the door and sits in a chair behind the director. In the rote silence that marks the beginning of every meeting, she looks at me, only me, and lights a cigarette.

She's going to share her five minutes with the entire staff. My secret of hers, out in the open. Like . . . like spreading her legs for the whole pack of them to take her.

The smoke reaches us one by one: first Ledesma and Mr. Allomby, followed by me and Papini, and then on to the rest in a chain that grows with each pull.

"Are you feeling all right, Quintana?" Ledesma asks.

"I'm fine."

"My dear colleagues," Ledesma says emphatically, "it's time to fail."

And so it begins. Some understand the reference to the anticipated "failure" of the serum, but others, less alert, part their lips, cough, and rub their noses in primitive bewilderment. Ledesma looks at them, pleased.

"We have enough patients to begin the exercise, and it would be a shame if they started dying on us first. A few of the more impatient ones already have. In my hand is a list of several individuals to whom we should propose donation. Since the subject is a bit dicey, if you'll pardon the pun, I took the liberty of laying out the process. If Doctor Gurian would be so kind as to read this . . ."

Gurian takes the stack of papers. Before he begins, he takes a moment to don his glasses and push the curls back from his forehead. I like Gurian, but I don't understand why they chose him when my voice is deeper, more resonant.

a)  *Failure*

*Failure resides simultaneously in two moments: when the individual establishes a goal, and when that goal is shown to be unattainable or specious. Oscillating between the goal and its ruin, searching for the error (failure is experienced as a defining quality), the individual's linear sense of time is shattered.*

*When they sign up for treatment, these patients declare a goal: to rid their body of cancer. Two months later, as could be expected, Dr. Beard's Serum has produced no results. We give them the bad news. A few will see the failure in the doctor's face; they will pity him and die peacefully. Most, however, will assume the failure as their own: "I am my cancer." Sparing them more of this misery in what remains of their lives, the doctor will use the donation to reestablish the patient's timeline in the form of a countdown.*

b)  *Indignity*

*The body is measured according to its utility. A good uterus, thriving progeny. Strong arms, men's work.*

*Lithe fingers, piano. Health is a prerequisite for the body's successful incorporation into the workings of the world. Illness devalues. How does one restore the dignity of the terminally ill? By returning their bodies to the realm of the useful, postmortem.*

c)  *Behavior toward the patient*

*On the day scheduled for the interview, the physician's brow should be clearly visible and pomade used sparingly. The patient will be shown in and offered tea or coffee. The unexpectedness of the gesture, so far from the conventions of a standard medical consultation, will prepare him to receive the terrible news: Dr. Beard's Serum is not working, and his demise is imminent. Once this news is on the table, a respectful silence will be observed while the patient does what he will with his pain.*

*The silence should not last for more than two minutes, at which time the doctor will stand up, cross the threshold of his desk, and touch the patient's back with one or both hands. If the patient resists this contact, the physician will make it clear that this gesture of compassion is not optional.*

d)  *Suitable communications*

*Having returned to his side of the desk, the physician will begin negotiations to acquire the body on behalf of Temperley Sanatorium. His tone should be deliberate and his phrasing, direct. It is recommended that he rehearse the conversation in advance, following these examples:*

*Correct phrasing: "Your body will help assure the well-being of future generations."*

*Incorrect phrasing: "Do it for your loved ones."*

> *Correct: "We appreciate your discretion."*
> *Incorrect: "Let's keep this between us."*
> *Correct: "Donate your body to science."*
> *Incorrect: "Donate yourself to science."*

e) *Discretion*

> *Once the consent of the patient, who will henceforth be referred to as the donor, has been secured, absolute discretion is required. He will be asked to sign a confidentiality agreement explaining that his body will be returned to his family in a closed casket and listing the laws that protect the experiment. These laws will be drafted by the sanatorium's owner, under the supervision of its director.*

> *If the donor has children for whom no one can take responsibility, a good-faith effort shall be made to ensure that the care of these future patriots does not fall into improvident hands. The sanatorium will assume responsibility for having them admitted to the appropriate state institution.*

> *Under no circumstances is the donor to be informed of the decapitation itself, or that the donation will occur pre-mortem.*

Gurian folds the papers and clears his throat. Ledesma explains that the rest of our instructions will be ready by Sunday, but that we should start clearing our consciences as soon as possible. He suggests confession or mass for the religious among us and acrobic exercise for the rest.

"We haven't tested the device on humans yet," he adds.

"But supposedly it works," says Gigena.

"So you've said," replies Ledesma.

"I don't know," Gigena says. "Are we moving too quickly?"

"Do we have the nuts to bake this cake or not?" Ledesma shouts. "They've got cancer! They're going to die anyway!"

Gigena breathes a sigh of relief because the outburst is directed at the group as a whole. The corners of Papini's mouth curve upward as if pulled by invisible wires.

"Ideas?" asks Mr. Allomby.

"That don't involve killing one of your colleagues," Ledesma jokes, having regained his composure.

Menéndez finishes her cigarette and looks for a place to stub it out. Mr. Allomby takes it from her gently, then looks her straight in the eye as he closes his fist around it, extinguishing it in his sweaty palm.

"You, Quintana." Ledesma points at me. "Tell us about that patient of yours, Sylvia."

"Who?" I come back to earth. "I don't have her clinical history on hand, but if you'd like . . ."

"If I'd like, what?" says Ledesma.

"Sylvia has no next of kin," Papini says, "and she's crazy as a loon. The rest of her is in mint condition, though, yes?" He looks at me.

I have no intention of answering.

"I don't think . . ." Sisman interjects, "I mean, who has the right to . . ."

"In theory, no one will notice she's gone," Papini continues.

"But, of course, there's the question of rights . . ." Ledesma says.

"Poor thing," says Gigena.

"Somebody grab that duck," Ledesma orders.

Sisman watches it scoot out from under the table. Getting down on all fours to catch it would be humiliating. He snaps his fingers, trying to call it over like a dog. Naturally, the animal ignores him. Gurian steps back, making it clear that the hunt is not at all his concern.

So who's going to bend over? Ledesma issued the order, and Mr. Allomby owns the sanatorium. Gigena is probably trying to find a solution favorable to both the duck and whoever catches it. Papini claps his hands.

"Menéndez," I say, looking her in the eye. "If you would."

"Doctor?"

I point at the duck.

Menéndez picks up the cigarette butt that Mr. Allomby left on the table after his little macho routine and offers it to the duck. The animal waddles over to her and swallows the detritus. She picks it up, walks out of the room, and doesn't look back.

"It's true, no one has the right to make that decision," says Ledesma. "But we could take a secret vote. All we need is a few slips of paper."

"I have a sheet right here," says Papini, extracting one from his pocket. "Scissors?"

"Just tear it," says Ledesma.

"There's no need to make this decision anonymously," Sisman interjects, "that is, if we're all real men."

"Let's leave our pants on, shall we?" Ledesma replies.

"The slips are ready," chirps Papini.

Put the paper on your lap and gaze into the distance, looking grim. Lift the pen and let it twitch in the air as if propelled by some heated internal dispute. I don't know what to write on mine. Sylvia's full name? An X? Yes or no? If so, yes to what? Everyone writes something except Mr. Allomby, who refused to take his slip. Papini, on the other hand, has two, and he weighs them with his eyes.

"Are you not voting, Mr. Allomby?" Sisman asks, crumpling his paper.

"Because I don't speak the Spanish well," Mr. Allomby replies.

I unfold the map of my options, spread them out. Whether I want to or not, I'm taking this seriously. Why wouldn't I want to? There are the low-risk options, the seat-of-your-pants options, the ones that mean there's no turning back, the false ones, the exit strategies. I'm among the stragglers—I, who always saw decisiveness as a manly quality, a strange ode to testosterone.

Using a map means paring it down to a line. I add my slip to the pile: fortunately, I'm not the last. Ledesma slides them all into a hat, shakes it up as if he were running a raffle, and takes them out one by one. He announces that, except for two abstentions, the decision is unanimous. The meeting is adjourned. Menéndez does not return.

I enter carrying a tray loaded with a slice of vegetable pie, a blood sausage, a quarter of a roast duck, an omelet, and a salad: a synthesis of all our meals from yesterday and today. I don't think Sylvia can eat it all. I prepare my face, adopt a friendly demeanor (I'm discharging her), show her the tray, and say, "For you," but the inveterate nutcase doesn't even give me the satisfaction of looking surprised—there's no occasion, no privilege, no last supper. I watch her eat in bed and serve her some wine.

In the morning we meet on the first landing of the main staircase. A nurse shows us up to the second. Then another nurse leads us into a waiting area, where we're offered coffee and a platter of biscuits that, for the moment, no one touches.

"I don't think Sylvia was the best choice," says Sisman.

"All that matters is that she says something," replies Gigena. "Otherwise, what's the point?"

They look at me. They're going to look at me every time they mention Sylvia.

"Do you know Doctor Iturralde?" Papini asks.

"No."

"I went to a party at his house last Saturday. It was the strangest thing: a man without a mustache walked right up to me and introduced himself as Mauricio."

The pause that follows is so conclusive, and lasts so long, that many of us get confused. Some even smile, celebrating the end of a great anecdote.

"I get to chatting with this fellow Mauricio," he continues, "who tells me about some land acquisition or another. Wheat fields, barley, your typical agricultural palaver. Then this fellow Mauricio introduces me to his brother, who's in the motion-picture business. Get this: his name is Mauricio, too. And it's not like one goes by Mauricio and the other uses a different name. It's the only one they have, and that's what everyone calls them. I bet more than one broad went nuts trying to explain to her girlfriends which one she liked."

He pauses again, longer than before. They look at him, waiting for him to go on. Papini whirls his hands, as if searching for something to add, until the ones who smiled last time smile again, shaking their heads.

Then we all hurry to grab a biscuit or two before they run out. Only a few eat theirs right away; most save them for later. We stand around in silence until a nurse tells us we can go downstairs.

We walk down the hallway to a door at the far end, on the other side of which are the stairs to the basement, and then to another door that opens onto the boiler room, and finally to the low-ceilinged room where the device is kept. I'm relieved not to be the first or last to enter.

Ledesma greets each of us by name, omitting the *Doctor.* Sylvia, sitting in her civilian attire with a cup of tea in her hand, indicates which chair each of us should take.

"How would you like to begin?" Ledesma asks us. "I'm open to suggestions."

"Let's cut right to the tenderloin," Sisman replies.

Mr. Allomby doesn't understand the phrase, and it takes us a while to explain the metaphorics of Argentine meat to him.

"Meat, slaughterhouses, death," says Ledesma. "Let's start with death. Let's say that in the course of all human experience, death is pure conjecture: it is, as such, not an experience. And all that which is not an experience is useless to mankind. Do you follow? Today we cast a flare into the great beyond to see what it illuminates in its flight. Is anyone taking notes?"

I raise my fountain pen and the notebook where I'll write down everything that happens from this moment on. At least, that's the arrangement Ledesma and I came to last week. My own secret arrangement, my real enterprise (hatred), will be to expand the territory of the report, decide where to begin, not to leave out Sylvia, or the ducks, or Menéndez; to be meticulous in my account but to avoid the mere accumulation of data. There will be plenty of time for me to expunge my personal journal from the experiment's.

Mr. Allomby seats Sylvia inside the device. There she is, curious, surrounded by men.

"All right, my dear," Ledesma says. "In a few minutes, I'm going to pull this lever here, you see? And the area around your neck might feel a little strange. Just stay calm, the way you do when Doctor Quintana gives you an injection."

"Doctor Quintana doesn't give me injections."

"No?" Ledesma looks at me. "What do you mean, he doesn't?"

"Sylvia was prescribed immersion therapy," I explain.

"But you must have injected her with something at some point."

Papini smiles, perfect lemon, in one of those agonizing triumphs he so enjoys. Has he really still not fixed that tooth?

"There was never any need for an injection."

"We'll discuss whether there was a need or not later, Quintana," Ledesma retorts, "but the fact that you never gave her an injection is a bit suspicious."

"Are you accusing me of something?"

"Do you feel like you're being accused of something, Quintana?"

"You're the director, and I would never question your staffing choices."

"We do have an enviable team."

"Absolutely."

"Of course."

Ledesma rests his hand on Sylvia's head. He asks her, clearly and deliberately, to tell us what she feels, sees, and hears after the strange sensation in her neck.

If the experiment is a success and Sylvia's head does indeed speak, I know it will say something about flies. I look forward to the widespread confusion, the frenzy of interpretations.

Sylvia nods, agreeing to cooperate as the two parts of the lid close around her neck and we fall silent. Ledesma pulls the lever. What follows is the contrast between the image constructed by expectation or fear and the sight of a head being neatly cleft from a torso. The blade moves quickly enough to neutralize the pain. An expression of mild discomfort flits across her face, a fluttering of the eyelids and a wrinkling of the nose that seems haughty, but is in fact just her respiratory system coming to an abrupt stop. This is the reaction noted in the first few seconds, then her pupils dilate and her jaw quivers.

Sylvia opens her mouth and emits an inhuman sound, the kind an automaton or a music box might make, with the air streaming past her vocal cords.

"*Sí,*" says the head. Her pupils constrict, and in the final second, her face is already the face of a dead woman.

"She said yes," whispers Papini.

"We forgot to call a priest," says Gigena, dabbing his forehead with a handkerchief.

"*Yes* what?" Ledesma snaps. "Did anyone ask her a question?"

"Unless it wasn't a *sí* like *yes*," Gurian says, ticking one finger upward in the air, "but rather the start, let's say, of a conditional statement. An *if,*" he adds, looking at Mr. Allomby, "a *si* without the accent."

"Let's not forget that she was crazy," Papini interjects.

"It was a success, in any event," Ledesma concludes. "What matters is that she said something."

"That's just what I suggested on the way in," Gigena asserts, ending the conversation.


A night on the town, courtesy of the sanatorium. Ledesma's plan includes cocktails, canapés, and ice-skating at the Palais de Glace, the only rink in South America. I read Menéndez's first name among the invited guests. She is the only single woman to be included in the outing, and I can guess by whom.

It's time to get back in the saddle. Being turned down for a cup of coffee is no obstacle for a gentleman in love. The pressure of a competition with Mr. Allomby and Papini could prove useful: knowing one's enemies, one can devise a proper strategy.

My enemy takes me by the arm and invites me to have a look around with him. There are curtains and people everywhere. A waiter offers us our first drink (we hear live music coming from somewhere) and comments that in a few years, the hall will likely be taken over by the tango. Mr. Allomby's face twists up in disgust, and he replies that by that time there will be better places to go.

In the crystalline cold I see Papini skating in circles, pure velocity and risk, almost endearing.

I wonder if that evening gown in Menéndez's closet will be brought out for the occasion. Menéndez. Menéndez. Her name ricochets around my body, shoots out of me like a rubber ball, and lands on the lips of Mr. Allomby, who utters it as if it were an exotic, prized object. He invites me to talk about her while we have a look at the works downstairs.

The basement is vast and has the same circular layout as the building above, but there are no dapper gents or ladies dancing demurely down here. Here there is manual labor, the dignity of hard work—a practical way to organize the space, but also an excessively literal reproduction of the world.

Men as stiff as butlers shovel coal into four steamboat boilers. The heat generates, first and foremost, a tremendous din: the whirring of reels and gears and pulleys (Mr. Allomby says the machine perfectly resembles a human body, but to me it's just a machine) converges at the ceiling, where the sound takes on the majesty of an echo. The heat also generates, wonder of wonders, the ice that covers the rink above us. We could have an interesting discussion about the fire-ice paradox, but we're two more drinks in and ready to swap confessions. Mr. Allomby tells me about a young woman from Southampton he seduced with a joke about a squid and a tennis champion. He is in the mood to take Menéndez and wants my advice. I suggest that he profess his love for her in front of everyone, out on the ice.

Gigena appears. He apologizes for his late arrival, describing his wife as a stupid mare. He stands beside Mr. Allomby, admiring what he describes as a technological symphony. Those are his exact words.

We stagger back to the main hall, smoking Havanas. We find the others at one of the tables. An empty seat prompts me to ask about Menéndez. She's in the bathroom. My mind turns to bidets.

Papini, propelled by the enthusiasm of someone seeing his friends arrive, crashes into the table, knocking over a glass. Mr. Allomby proposes that we follow his example and take a spin around the ice. Ledesma is first to his feet, and the rest immediately follow suit.

We step onto the ice. This is how I want to remember us: dressed in formal black, doctoral mustaches, masculine aura, skating in circles, not saying a word. We've fallen into the silence of concentration, of deliberate enjoyment. And we move with grace.

Menéndez returns and watches us dispassionately from her seat. Mr. Allomby does an undignified pirouette, musters his courage, and approaches, inviting her to join him on the ice. In the time it takes her to get her skates laced up, I strategize countermeasures and then give in to physical instinct: I accelerate my lap, risking a fall that would ruin everything, pass Mr. Allomby, and offer my hand to the tremulous head nurse, who's just stepped onto the rink. In one fell swoop, I (a virile

Quintana, a charging Quintana) pull her away from the railing, gathering her up in my movement. She depends entirely
on me.

Mr. Allomby follows close behind, holding onto the railing; Papini and Gurian skate up to him, take an arm each,
and guide him toward us. He smiles first at me and then at
Menéndez before using us as a bumper to halt his trajectory.
He kneels on the ice.

The others gather in, tightening the circle around us. I'm
spinning, too, so it almost looks like they're standing still.
Menéndez opens her mouth to say something (but I thought
you only responded?) and Mr. Allomby starts gushing a pro-
logue that telegraphs his intentions from the outset, trying to
make his voice sound deeper, like a schoolboy with his first
whore. Somehow he manages to use words like "angel" and
"nuptials" without sounding contemptible. He says that his
love is pure and he doesn't expect an immediate answer, only
an "I'll think about it."

The applause builds, centrifugal, overflowing the circle of
ice and surging up the stairs. In its center, Menéndez is con-
densed, made material; she adopts her decisive form. If one
were to break a glass on her forehead, she would bleed.

She doesn't say a word. She isn't even really looking at
him. The applause dies down. Mr. Allomby realizes that he's
kneeling on the ice, ruining his pants, that his face is bright
red, that he might have to wait forever for an answer, and that
this scene will be relived behind his back until the day of his
suicide, if not longer. He grabs my waist and hauls himself
to his feet, then pulls me out of the circle without dampen-
ing my perfect, nearly spastic, happiness. I realize we won't
be taking off our ice skates, and we scratch our way across the
parquet floors toward the bathroom. His palms are frosted

with sweat and leave halos on my jacket; with every step, he feels like more of a burden.

We step into the bathroom. Someone is crying in one of the stalls. As I steady a vomiting Mr. Allomby, I examine the sufferer's shoes in the mirror. I'm less interested in figuring out who he is than I am in understanding how he could have so little shame. Mr. Allomby is weeping, too, as he awaits the next wave of nausea.

I ask loudly if anyone else needs assistance. The stall door opens and Sisman shows his face, red with anguish.

I'm the only one who isn't crying. With no small measure of fear I think, I'm not capable of that much grief.

# 3

No one has seen her since that night at the Palais. They say she's locked herself in her room. The nurses lack confidence in her absence. Menéndez was kind enough to prepare a schedule outlining every single task that needs to be done over the next two days, but they don't trust the written word.

I finish reading Sisman's letter. It explains why he was crying in the Palais, how he wants to die, and why it seems fitting *to follow Sylvia* in one of the sanatorium's rooms. Those are his exact words.

It takes me a moment to realize that a colleague's life is in my hands. That there's still time to save him.

As I reread certain passages, a staff nurse sees him enter a room, slamming the door behind him. She is struck by his pallor and the blue of his lips. She knocks and asks if everything is all right, to which Sisman replies with a scream that wakes the entire sanatorium. His scream also interrupts my perusal of the note, which I tuck away in my pocket.

During the rescue, I want so badly to tell everyone that I could burst. But the story of how Sisman fell in love with Sylvia, maintained a secret relationship with her, promised to get her discharged, and then participated in her decapitation is just too juicy for a summary. I decide to save it for afternoon tea.

Sisman wants us to leave him alone. We ask him not to go through with it. Who's stronger? The door doesn't give; we bounce off it like rubber balls. Gigena takes the lead with surprising force. Ledesma charges, leading with his torso. Gurian is still trying the lock.

Rubbing his shoulder as he declines his turn, Papini wonders out loud what might have prompted Sisman to leave his suicide note in my office.

"Quintana's trustworthy!" Sisman shouts from inside.

When we make it inside, Sisman is trying to squeeze himself through the window. Blue pills are scattered around an overturned glass on the gurney. Ledesma brings him down with one tug. He falls into our arms with a sudden calm that makes our blood run cold.

We lay him down on the gurney and race through the halls. The cancer cases are moved by the scene and lean forward despite the risk that the tubes might fall out of their arms. The institution's image changes in our wake. One nurse takes the reins and points us toward the operating room, confusing the situation with an emergency surgery. It will do for now.

Ledesma asks me for the note. He reads it in front of Sisman as if it were a clinical history. When he reaches the part that alludes to Sylvia, he continues in silence and suggests we withdraw to give the patient some air. Sisman opens his blue mouth, lies agape like that for a moment, then asks me to stay. I close the operating room doors on my colleagues' curiosity, ordering them to get ready to pump his stomach.

"This is a pretty nasty surprise, Sisman," Ledesma says.

"I never took advantage of her. I'm not a piece of shit," Sisman replies.

"Would you like some water?"

"What makes you think I'm thirsty?"

"Because you're gulping air like a little fish."

"Leave me alone."

"Give him a glass of water, Quintana." Ledesma sighs. "I'm a man just like you are, Sisman. We're all men here. We understand one another. This Sylvia business stays between us."

"We're all men here? I'm not so sure," says Sisman.

"True." Ledesma rubs his eyes. "There might be a poof hiding among us."

"Who?" I ask.

"I don't know who. But someone could turn fairy on us at any moment—it's been known to happen—especially at such a critical time for the sanatorium."

"Go fuck yourselves," Sisman says, listless.

"Give him a little slap, Quintana."

This kind of order doesn't seem strange to me anymore. The string coils in my hand and snaps against Sisman's face.

"You do realize that once we've pumped your stomach we're going to have to fire you," Ledesma says.

"I just took eight Parvenol I'll give you one guess whether I give a shit about this fucking place."

"Eight Parvenol won't get you anywhere, Sisman. By tomorrow, you'll be eating a steak dinner. Behave yourself, and I'll make sure you get a good severance package."

"I don't care."

"You have no reason to kill yourself here."

"I want to be with her, don't you get it?"

"You want a selfish death."

"I don't care what kind it is."

"Let's talk, then "

"You can have my head," says Sisman.

"Once you've recovered," Ledesma replies.


A few days later, the groundskeeper's shed catches fire again. The night shift observes the blaze, noting that bad luck tends to come in threes. Ledesma, more practical than intrigued, says we need to find the pyromaniac before he destroys something more expensive or harder to replace. The flames lap at the nearest tree. A delightful scent filters between our faces.

Sisman is a gentleman; he doesn't come at me with embraces or pats on the back. He walks calmly a few paces ahead. With aplomb. He lights a cigarette, leaving a trail I can follow down the length of the hall without having to keep him in sight.

He closes his office door quietly. On the floor are several leather suitcases and a wooden crate. He tells me they contain all his worldly possessions. It doesn't seem like very much. Maybe he was bad with money. I don't know. I don't know anything about him. I deduce that he's a loner: he considers me his closest friend.

I ask (to be polite) whether he plans to donate his things to charity. He replies indifferently that he plans to burn them in the sanatorium furnace so he can go without leaving a trace. He points to the crate.

"I want you to keep this, Quintana."

The prospect of having a lasting reminder of Sisman in my life worries me. I feel like I'm being asked to carry a relic, the hand or torso of a saint.

"It's my collection of frogs," he says. "Five hundred frogs."

I leave them on my desk. The frogs are made of metal and each is no bigger than a nut. They're painted bright green and have two slots where their eyes should be. If you press their back legs down with one finger, they spring up in the air and a little bell inside them rings; the high-pitched noise continues when they return to the ground, making them easier to find. Sisman says they're toys for blind children. He sets off a row of them with a sweeping movement of his hand. How? As if from a speeding train.

Mr. Allomby leans on the device, bracing himself with both hands. His face is damp. He says something incomprehensible. Who would dare to correct his Spanish? We're all just as tired as he is. It shows in the dark circles under our eyes; we slept on gurneys until it was time. No one helps him up. Mr. Allomby takes a breath, brushes the hair back from his forehead, and asks Sisman to please just take his seat inside the device.

"I'd like to say a few words first," says Sisman.

"Get on with it," Ledesma replies.

Sisman looks at the device. A few of us think he's going to chicken out at the last minute, while others expect him to make some brief, trivial remarks to prove he's not a coward.

"There's nothing extraordinary about suicide," he begins.

"Why deny it?" Ledesma interrupts

"But this one is different. A collaborative suicide. You have no idea how good it feels."

Someone applauds. I don't know who; he's behind me. Another follows suit, so as not to leave him hanging. We applaud. Sisman thanks us and takes his seat inside the device. Ledesma closes the lid around his neck.

"Thank you, Doctor," he says, enthusiastic.

Ledesma does not pull the lever right away. The blade slices through the doctor, though not as smoothly as in Sylvia's case. His head moves an inch across the lid and off the vent, making it impossible for him to speak. Ledesma spends the first two seconds putting it back in place. Sisman's eyes open wide and his nostrils flatten until the air starts running through them again. At no point does it look like he's trying to open his mouth. Because he doesn't speak, the process seems to go more quickly, as if he'd died right there on the spot.

Ledesma brings his fist down hard on the device.

"Go get some rest," he says.

I see Papini trying out his speech on a patient. I walk over and stand next to him, apologizing for the interruption. I pretend to look over some papers. How much courtesy is required when asking someone for their body? I want to see his solution. It's Papini's first time (his nervousness has no specific odor), and he is mute in my presence.

"I don't understand," says the patient.

"The serum isn't producing the desired result," says Papini.

"I can wait for it to start working."

"No. It's not working. It's not going to work."

"Are you sure?"

Papini doesn't have a scientific face. He has freckles. No diploma in the world can make freckles disappear. I look at him as one would look at a colleague, but with the same reservations as the patient. Are you sure, Papini?

"If you'd like, you can request a consultation."

"A consultation? What's that?"

"Doctor Quintana is right here." He points a flaccid finger at me. "Ask him, if you like."

"I can't offer an opinion without seeing the tests," I say, my exit strategy at the ready.

"They're right there on the desk, Quintana." I catch a strong whiff of lemon.

I do have a scientific face and can opine without raising suspicions.

"The serum isn't producing the desired result," I say to Papini, without looking at the patient.

"There are bodies, and there are bodies," Papini says.

"But why not mine?" asks the patient.

"It's a matter of chemistry," I say firmly. "Too much potassium in yours, perhaps. You're of Italian origin, correct? Southern Italy?"

"Yes," says the patient.

"Mediterranean climate, lots of sun," I continue, politely now. "Mother Nature is wise, and she endowed you southern Italians with high levels of potassium to protect you from the climate there. Unfortunately—unfortunately, indeed— potassium affects the chemical structure of Beard's Serum. That's the point. Do you understand?"

The patient doesn't understand, but it's enough for him that I do; meanwhile, he's busy asking himself why he had the bad luck to be born in Italy and how he can avoid going to hell after thinking such terrible things about God.

"I'd like to discuss an opportunity with you," says Papini.

"I have another consultation in five minutes," I say. I know it's not an elegant exit, but so what. "I'll leave you to it."

"Thanks, Doc," the patient says.

His error of diction hastens my exit. That kind of thing can throw me off for several minutes.

"What will you do with my body?" is the most common question, grounded not so much in a shortage of nobility or interest in the greater good as in an excess of mistrust. The answer demands creativity. Experiments with cold and heat; donations of lungs, heart, corneas; conservation of the skin; anything, really—so long as it doesn't involve heads.

Gurian hits a virtuosic note when, betting on the perfect ignorance of his interlocutor, he promises a postmortem study of the circulatory system. If he's accused of talking nonsense, he simply smiles and describes a device that is, essentially, a vacuum pump designed to reactivate the circulation of the deceased.

Most of them allow themselves to be convinced because they intuit that Argentina is tackling a scientific challenge of global proportions; in this patriotic fervor, they sign over their bodies. The air of historical significance lends itself to an easy yes.

We note down the donations on a chart Menéndez hands us at the end of each interview. Its design puts us on the offensive: next to the donor's name and the estimated delivery date, one field demands the surname of the doctor who acquired the body. The next few years in the sanatorium, the possibility of professional advancement, and perhaps even a friendship with Mr. Allomby—who will be measuring our aptitude as doctors and human beings based on these results—depend on how often our names appear. The number must not be negligible.

Gigena leads by two donations. People leave his office smiling. Papini's cancer cases walk out wondering if they've done the right thing. Mine leave convinced but taciturn—not even sad, really—with absolute faith in the institution and concrete plans for their last will and testament.

Those who refuse our offer rise from their chairs with the elegance of a mantis, convey their sadness at the serum's failure as they shake our hands, and close the door quietly as they leave.

Ledesma underestimates the plan's greatest flaw: the massive failure of our cancer treatment will mean a shortage of future patients and fewer heads for the device. How are we supposed to get donations without undermining the credibility of the bait?

In good spirits, Ledesma proposes more or less respectable accidents (a streetcar collision rather than simply being run over) so the cancer cases die from something other than their disease and don't call the efficacy of the serum into question. Ideally, according to him, we would find the real cure by asking the heads to snatch the formula right out from under God's nose.

Mr. Allomby believes that when the decapitations begin, God will be able to share his Word with us using the heads as a megaphone.

Behind his back, Gurian says that Mr. Allomby is hoping for a religious epiphany and to pay cash for a plot in the hereafter. *Cash,* he says, in English.

Ledesma asks if we've been baptized, rolls his eyes skyward, and proclaims that if God does anything, it'll be to hightail it the hell out of here. He says *high tail.*

This time, Menéndez tosses her half-smoked cigarette, lifts her head, and stares straight at me. My first impulse is to step away from the window, but my body brings me back on its own, as if offended by my cowardice. I return her gaze with a look that says "So what?" while she lowers her eyes as if nothing has happened.

I should formulate a partial, convenient interpretation of that gaze. Reach her before she gets back to work. Without breaking into a run, but quickly. Call her in and lay out my intentions, one by one.

I head downstairs. I'm wearing nice shoes.

Why like this? Why not a simpler way? What does it take, on average, to make a woman fall in love? Anyone who sees it as a matter of minutes or days is failing to consider their intricacies, their traceries—what Papini calls *the threat.*

Menéndez stands behind the team of nurses. I catch sight of her before she evaporates among the others. I point at her from the far end of the hallway and call her by her first name. She approaches with the air of someone about to correct an error or request an explanation. Now everyone in earshot knows her name. They can use it to gain her trust or say it softly, as if talking about a dear friend. She exists in a tangible, demonstrable sense. And it's my fault. Her name is the lance tied to the string coiled in my hand.

"I need you to wait for me in my office, Menéndez."

"Now, Doctor?"

"Now."

She knows the order has to do with the way she stared straight at me. She's busy but agrees. I watch her go. Let her wait there, with my things. In the unwritten rules of amorous conquest, waiting is a key element. And it gives me time to figure out what I'm going to say and how, which of my voices I'll use, which gestures.

I unfold the map of my options, spread them out. Whether I want to or not, I'm taking this seriously. Why wouldn't I want to?

Open the door, slam my fist on the desk, and say, "I love you." Act like a doctor and invite her to coffee. Can that be done twice? Walk in, invent some complicated task that puts her back in her preferred role momentarily, then toss in a personal comment and see if it leads to a more candid, delicate chat. Or do the truly heroic thing: accuse her of trying to seduce me.

I crash into these specters one by one. And there's Papini, crystal clear among them.

"Did you hear the news, Quintana?"

"No."

"Not very dedicated, are we?"

He wants to lose another tooth. If he appeals to my generosity, he'll probably get his wish. But first, there's something he wants to confess. I can smell it on him. Why do people insist on confessing things to me? Must be something in my face. As we walk, I wonder what faces might inspire my confessions. Men's faces? Women's?

Menéndez must be sitting across from my empty chair with her legs pressed tightly together, or looking out my window to see what I see when I spy on her, or else following my order to wait, patiently and without secrets.

"They let me measure Sisman," Papini says. "Atavistic. He kept it hidden, but he was. Look at that dome! Ledesma was so shocked he ordered me to measure all the donors from now on. What do you make of that?"

"Congratulations, Papini. What are you going to do with the donors who don't pass the test?"

"We can't dash their hopes of participating. But we have to consider the circumstances. It wouldn't be wise to take a primate's word about the existence of the hereafter."

"Since when are we trying to prove that?"

"I'm speaking figuratively, Quintana."

"Is there anything else I can do for you?"

"Do you know where Menéndez is?" He is immediately aware of his error, of the risk to his teeth. "My interest is strictly professional, of course."

"Menéndez is waiting for me in my office."

I smile at him like someone who smiles all the time.

Menéndez's time, thus suspended, belongs to me, but I approach my office unsure of what to do with it, or her. Making her wait any longer would mean transforming her anticipation into boredom, but to walk in and stand there stammering would be failure itself—worse than Mr. Allomby's scene on the ice. He was tragic, at least. I would just be inarticulate.

I stand at the door and observe her through the glass stamped with my name: the most banal partition imaginable between a man and his enigmatic beloved. She stands stiff, with her head held high. The hallway light casts the shadow of my surname across her forehead.

I walk in and close the door. I catch a whiff of cigarette smoke—her second today. Her routine does not include second cigarettes.

"This is outrageous," she says. "I've wasted twenty minutes waiting here for you, when I could be in my room, resting, or doing something useful. You go too far, Quintana. Just like the rest of them."

Tears fill my eyes. Menéndez sits behind my desk in my chair and points a finger at me.

"You little weasels. Did anyone think to ask if I wanted to be part of this? I don't care that you're cutting off people's heads. But lying to cancer patients just seems . . ."

She means to say immoral, but she makes a mistake and says something else. I'd like to be able to correct her.

"I don't talk much," Menéndez continues. "You and your colleagues know this about me. It's probably all you know. But I never agreed to any of this. Can you get that into your head? Because if not, I quit."

"You can't quit, Menéndez. Don't quit. Please."

"And why not?"

"I love you, Menéndez."

I don't pause as long as I should.

"But if I don't get a chance to get to know you before . . . even if only a little, if you go . . . Don't go. I'm a good guy. I only want the best for you. I'm only asking you to think about it."

"I know you're in love with me. Do you think that's some kind of excuse? Why are you crying? Explain yourself, sir!"

I look out the window. The circle of ants is still perfect. Menéndez stands, knowing that I will not explain myself and that she went too far in her role as the Offended Young Lady.

"Balls, Quintana," she says.

She looks for an ashtray to stub out her cigarette, but there isn't one and she exits my office carefully, trying to keep the ash from falling. And with that punctilious gesture, she's gone.

Balls. What to do with those? Menéndez's parting words assure me that I still have a chance (she didn't say no), but until I can figure out what she was trying to say, where to put them, there will be no Menéndez, and no virile Quintana: he left my office in the palm of her hand and fell with her cigarette ash.

Ledesma announces that the experiment will begin within the next few days. We raise our glasses. He claims to envy the donors because, for nine seconds, *the Truth will be of them.* He corrects himself and changes Truth to Abundance, then trades Abundance for Spectacle, still insisting on the capitalization. But he feels he hasn't quite found the right phrase. He reasons that, in the thrall of Glory (Mr. Allomby repeats the word as if to confirm it's the right one, so it sticks) the heads will require an external stimulus if they are to deign to share their stories. He underscores that our role in the Glory will be to make ourselves a nuisance. To mitigate this effect, the questions should be selected with great care.

What should we ask? Avoid yes-or-no questions. Avoid questions that require more than ten or twelve words to formulate; according to his calculations, this is all we have time for. Avoid questions that rely on or encourage the use of metaphor. Avoid questions that employ complex vocabulary, that might send a head short on brains into crisis. Avoid questions involving the terms *God, heaven, science,* and, understandably, *head.*

I look at Menéndez. Surrounded by men. Shielded by everything they don't know about her. But I know more. At the very least, I know about the second cigarette that represents the limit of her patience. Which is precisely why she refuses to look at me now.

As an amusing digression, Gigena invites us in a didactic tone to consider the issue of nomenclature.

"Is the severed head still Juan or Luis Pérez, to pull a name out of a hat, or does it become *the head of Juan or Luis Pérez?*"

The question, which concerns me directly (I keep the written record of the experience), reminds me that Papini's mother's leg has its own headstone.

Everyone looks at me. Menéndez looks at me for the first time since the meeting began. I sense that she wants me to give an answer worthy of my intentions with her. That she wants it doesn't matter. She deserves it. And so, just like that, I find myself in the bind of needing, essentially, to be brilliant. My balls aren't exactly on the line, but it should be clear that I'm a man of ideas, that I can call them up at will, should the occasion arise.

"The notion of Juan or Luis Pérez is a complex one," I say, praying my argumentation improves as I go on, "which includes arms, lungs, a heart . . . so much of Juan-or-Luis

Pérez rests in his organs. Is it his brain that flutters when he falls in love? Is it really the brain that loosens our bowels when we get scared? Show some humility, gentlemen. When we drink wine, are we the ones who choose to knock the whole glass back in one swallow, or is it our throats? When we go visit our mothers, it may well be our feet that make the decision and then project a map of our trajectory onto our brains. Consequently, as far as I'm concerned, once the blade does its work, Juan-or-Luis Pérez is no more and what we have is a *head,* with functions limited to those of a head."

"For Pete's sake," Gurian says.

"I don't know, Quintana," Ledesma says. "I don't know. I'm not interested in having a conversation with anyone's liver. I'd rather believe that Juan or Luis Pérez's head is still more or less him."

"Without question," Papini says.

We debate whether to ask the questions before or after the decapitation. Do we want to guide the responses? Some, quite reasonably, prefer not to. Ledesma squints. He's in favor of a postmortem questionnaire. He contends we'll get the most diaphanous responses that way. Mr. Allomby doesn't understand the word, and no one steps up right away to translate it for him.

"If our questions lead the donor to suspect we're about to cut off his head," Ledesma continues, "he'll feel like he's being conned and will necessarily tend toward fear and that loosening of the bowels that Doctor Quintana mentioned. One is unlikely to encounter the Glory under those conditions. And also, gentlemen, common sense: we don't want them having second thoughts at the last minute. That one's on the house."

"Let's not ask questions," says Gurian. "Let the heads speak for themselves."

There is something liberating in his proposal, so we defend it against Ledesma's and Mr. Allomby's rebukes. The bodies and their diseases belong to the patients, sure, but we're the ones who have to smell their innards, and if things go badly, we're the ones who'll take the blame. If things go well, on the other hand, God gets all the credit.

To be present, but not participate directly, is the dream of every doctor.

By the end of the discussion, Ledesma has conceded every point, but he reserves the right to ask questions if he so desires. A director reserving the right to do anything is such a pathetic redundancy that we lose respect for him on the spot.

"Well, that's settled," Ledesma says. "Now we can move on to announcing the names of the three doctors who earned a bonus for securing the most donations. The list, please, Menéndez."

No one said the results would be made public in such a humiliating way. Or mentioned any bonus. Many of us probably took the whole thing lightly because of that. The sweat from our necks trickles down to our asses; if it weren't for our underwear, it would continue all the way down to our feet and gradually form a puddle big enough to swim in. It won't be long before some of them lose their offices and others move on to bigger ones, far from the pus and malaria.

In first place: the doctor with the mole on his chin. He receives a round of incredulous applause from those of us who know nothing about him, not even his name, which, incidentally, we drowned out with our applause.

Gigena has the good taste to come in second, which allows him to demonstrate his competence while avoiding the cloying scent of victory.

"There's a tie for third place," Ledesma continues. "I don't say it's a tie because this is a competition, understand? But simply because two of your colleagues ended up with the same number of donations, and our budget won't accommodate four bonuses."

I'd like to come in fourth: the best among the losers. Ledesma announces that Papini and I share third place. He applauds us for going onto the field of battle hand in hand. Those are his exact words.

We have two days to get more donors. Papini is already imagining fifteen horrible strategies for seducing more cancer cases than me. I look at Menéndez and dedicate the fifteen balls of my imminent triumph to her. Her love is of the kind that can be claimed through grand gestures. Underappreciated testosterone.

The patient as a number: nothing new there, but now there's a prize involved. I have five donations. As I go for my sixth, a woman laughs in my face. For my seventh, I approach the donor and try to console him by resting a hand on his head; it ends up smeared with pomade. My ninth is tricky: the donor faints before signing. I bring him to with alcohol, papers in hand, because no one is watching.

Ledesma slams the chart down on his desk and asks Papini who the donor that doesn't appear on the list of patients is. I shoot Mr. Allomby a conspiratorial glance. We're not actually conspiring, but it's important to look at people like that every now and then because that's how real relationships are forged.

"It's Mauricio Albano Ruiz, sir," Papini replies. "Do you remember my anecdote about the brothers Mauricio?"

"No."

"The one in the motion-picture business. He came to the sanatorium last week to visit me. And do you know what? He told me that the movement we see on the screen is all a lie. There's no movement. It's photographs. Get it? Like a zoetrope! How many photographs per second do you think it takes for the movement to look fluid, natural? I'm taking bets. What do you say? And how about you, Mr. Allomby?"

"I don't care," says Mr. Allomby.

"How many?"

"I don't know," Mr. Allomby replies, annoyed. "A hundred, more or less."

"No one knows! That's the problem. Mauricio tried to figure out the magic number so he could patent it in Argentina. He's been working on it for years. Seems they've already solved the mystery in France or the United States, but they're keeping it hush-hush. The most remarkable thing, the most charming part, I'd say, is that while Mauricio was chasing real time, his own time ran out."

"What are you talking about, Papini?"

"Literally, his time ran out. He's so discouraged he wants to die. He asked to participate in the experiment."

"I appreciate your dedication, but I can already see this Mauricio fellow at some cocktail party, tossing out the details of this experiment that has cost us so dearly to play up his eccentricity or impress some young lady. No, Papini. Mr. Mauricio will keep his head for now, and so will you."

Papini finds Ledesma's joke hilarious and concedes the competition. I win a bonus for my tally of twelve donors to eleven, not counting Mauricio.

"But this Mr. Albano Ruiz knows about the experiment," I add. "He might talk anyway. Especially if he feels he's been slighted."

"That's the attitude I like to see in my staff," says Ledesma. "Thank you."

"Please, let's approve the head," says Papini. "Doctor Quintana's bonus is not under dispute."

Papini's spirit has been forged in failure. A few more like this and he might even be tolerable. He comes up short as a leading man, but he's a hero nonetheless. Mr. Allomby ends the meeting by saying they'll only accept Mauricio's head in exchange for a substantial sum. One shouldn't make things easy for the upper class.

Menéndez hands me the envelope with my bonus. The principal breakthrough in our relationship is that she's traded her anger for total indifference. The next step must be love.

How many words do we say in a year? The figure matters to no one, least of all me, but it's surprising that it doesn't appear in the *Encyclopædia Britannica*. One possible explanation is that no one listens carefully. What remains of us as time passes are our words, sure, but in abridged form, crossed out according to the interest they hold for others. It's different for these poor creatures. We're going to listen to them meticulously.

Ledesma wears a bow tie in the national colors and reads an inaugural speech full of suspense, zeal, and opportune digressions. On each chair—an essential detail—rests a slip of paper with one of our names on it. We don't know if the assignments are random or if they correspond to how important we are. Menéndez stands a few paces from the device.

The first donor is Elsa: fifty-two years old, pancreatic cancer, widowed housewife, childless. I write her name like an insignia. When the experiment reaches its mythic stage, we'll be able to look back on our primordial Elsa. Ledesma offers his hand and seats her in the device.

"How are you feeling?"

He activates the blade before the question is fully formulated. Elsa doesn't notice.

*"Been better,"* the head replies in a monotone. *"The ceiling is really low."*

The first two seconds pass like this. Ledesma tosses out a "You think so?" that occupies the third, and the head adds nothing in the time that remains. The transition from one state to the other was so abrupt that some bit of "Elsahood" could have lingered in the head. Eternity doesn't know from low ceilings. It's a good phrase to present later, playing devil's advocate—the embodiment of dedication to any cause.

Then comes the next one, with a different name.

"Relax, sir," says Ledesma, activating the blade.

*"What did you do to my neck?"* asks the head.

"Nothing."

*"I'm not sure . . ."* the head says, in closing.

Gurian reminds us that our policy is not to ask questions. Ledesma brings in the third donor, seats him in the device, and says nothing as he pulls the lever.

The face twists up in pain. The mouth opens and, taking advantage of the current of air provided by the device, screams for nine seconds straight. One of my colleagues faints: he blanches for seconds one through nine, then falls silently to the floor without overturning his chair. It takes us a while to revive him. Ledesma suggests he step out for some air, but he's stubborn and takes his seat again.

The next donor is shown in. A young woman, about twenty years old. I wonder who's in charge of the bodies stacking up in the storage room. Papini has a habit of touching the breasts of unconscious old ladies. What's to stop him from doing the same with this girl's body later, when no one is watching? If he were capable of that, though, Menéndez would already be his. He's not capable of that.

"Can I ask a question?" says the girl.

"By all means," replies Ledesma.

"The donation happens after I die, right?"

"Of course," says Ledesma. "Have a seat."

The girl wants to say something else, but Mr. Allomby pulls the lever.

*"I'd like some water,"* says the head.

If faith demands that each answer be an epiphany, then the Whole is not unlike this time, this space. Or perhaps our gaze has rested so intently on things that it's taken on their form, their weight, their duration—immutably: one single habit, one continuous hat wrapping around heads, even across worlds.

In either case, a cosmic disappointment. If *intellectual honesty* indicates, on the other hand, that waiting for an epiphany inherently means accepting failure, well then, there's still time—not to abort the experiment, but rather to assign it a new goal. The next donor will separate the wheat from the chaff: some will cling to faith, others will not.

Ledesma can smell our disappointment. It oozes from his pores, too. But there's no reason to read the device like tea leaves. We'll draw our conclusions when we have more heads. Mr. Allomby proposes a snack break.

I can't help being the first to get up, so all eyes fall on me. Some assume I'm craving a sandwich, and their mouths start to water too, though they remain seated. Others think I'm losing my nerve and want to get away from the experiment as quickly as possible. I slow my pace to avoid arousing more suspicion.

At this reduced pace, I see Mr. Allomby take Menéndez by the arm, as if the spectacle at the Palais never happened, as if she'd agreed to let him start with a clean slate. He guides her toward the door. They're talking about something I can't quite make out. I hurry.

"I'll think about it, Mr. Allomby," Menéndez says.

"Thank you."

They smile at each other.

Of course. A snap of the fingers. Life goes on for her, while I'm breaking my back to prove something or other about my balls. The enemy does not rest; he's taken aim and fired off a proposal, the second, far from the public gaze of a ballroom, in a hallway Menéndez knows like the back of her hand, where she feels comfortable and barely visible.

Do you see this shoelace? I'd like to take it and tie your tongue to your uvula, and your uvula to your stomach, and your stomach to your uterus, so that the very first word of your answer leaves you hollow.

My mouth is full of ham and cheese. If I were to open it, you wouldn't be able to see my teeth. I'm chewing like one of those derelict immigrants who stuff their faces down by the docks, planning crimes against the very society that welcomed them to this promised land. I chew like a man with a fearsome jaw, like that other ape I'm about to unleash.

Ledesma is playing with a coin, tossing it in the air and catching it without looking. My colleagues consider this worthy of praise. The director is so talented, so whimsical. In this momentary suspension of the hierarchy, opportunists come out of the woodwork. They force their way in through the cracks of minor passions (parlor games, married life, some remark of Gurian's about fencing), convinced that working their way up the ladder begins with winning over the man. The knowing wink. It's so outrageously naïve I could beat them to a bloody pulp.

The practical, indirect Quintana, that peddler of ambiguities, ends here. What was I waiting for? For time to balance the scales? For chance to intervene? For the magic of love? I stride over to Ledesma without wiping my mouth and, defying my (let's call it) nature, deftly thrust my arm forward to grab the coin midair. I need to talk to him. Now. Alone.

He wants to see how I do it. I have his approval but not his confidence. We go together to find our next donor: one of those men who is thought to have sound judgment because he wears a clean suit. I don't separate him from the others or offer him a seat. I tell him the donation will occur while he is still alive and that the sanatorium will administer his death. That his head will be severed from his body painlessly, or that the pain will be fleeting compared to dying of cancer, and that for nine seconds he will have an experience so intense that time will seem relative. That this internal temporal elasticity will allow him to narrate what he observes to us, in appreciation of the great gift we're offering him, so that the revelation (we expect nothing less) can be of use to those of us who remain among the living. The epic language I use makes him cross his arms. After a moment, during which Ledesma asks himself why he'd agreed to this in the first place, the man stretches his neck to stand a bit taller and says, "Why not?"

The donor takes his seat in the device, serene because I have assigned him a higher purpose. Ledesma reflects on my intelligence, my fearlessness. Are you listening, Menéndez?

"As you will recall," says Ledesma, "my original proposal relied on the donor's ignorance. And, as no one challenged me on this"—he raises an admonishing finger—"we began the exercise under those terms. We are all aware of the results. But Doctor Quintana, whose dedication is beyond reproach, put on his thinking cap and proposed a new strategy, which we're about to put to the test. Tell them, boss."

That "boss" is worth several bonuses, but I feel like a small child being forced to play piano or recite a poem for distant relatives. I ready my deepest voice.

"If the donor doesn't know what awaits him," I say, "he will be entirely focused on processing the surprise of what has just happened to his neck rather than thinking in terms of a higher objective."

"The hard part is conveying this information with care and dignity," Ledesma says.

"As if that were so hard," says Papini. "We do it every day. We did it with Beard's Serum."

"It's not the same," Ledesma replies. "I challenge you to ask someone for his head. Just watch what happens. How do you present the idea without causing the donor pain that could cloud his judgment? It requires tremendous sangfroid, tremendous scientific vocation, not mincing like a sissy. Look how skillfully Quintana overcame that obstacle! What's your opinion, sir?"

"Doctor Quintana gave it to me straight," the donor says. "Always appreciate that. Me, I'm right as rain."

"A round of applause for our donor," Gigena says.

We applaud. I see doubt flash across a few faces. Do they think I'm heartless? I'm more sensitive than all of you, but that won't help me win Menéndez, and this grabbing the bull will, I think, because she's the last one to stop clapping.

"Give us your best," says Ledesma as he pulls the lever.

*"There are people who don't exist,"* the head asserts, its eyes half-closed.

This is where it begins. The mark of the real Quintana. A perfect phrase for this parade of hypotheses. And although there are those who would argue it means nothing (as I myself would do, were my new role of go-getter not at stake), the amazement is contagious. It's all Mr. Allomby can do not to start clapping like a jubilant peasant woman. Ledesma pounds a fist on the device and lets out an "All right!" that fills us with common enthusiasm. If we had hats, we'd be tossing them in the air.

"We can understand the phrase in one of two ways," Papini says. "One: from his perspective, we do not exist. In other words, we are anchored in time and therefore invisible to him, as he is already in Eternity. Two: his perspective allows him to see something we cannot, and this *something* was with us in the form of a spectral presence during those nine seconds."

"*Something,* presented in those terms, is not a verifiable object," Gurian objects. "As such, I suggest changing course before the discussion is derailed."

"Let's not start setting up roadblocks," says Ledesma.

"There is a third possibility," Papini continues. "His atemporal perception allows him to see us as we were, are, will be, and even *could* be. He looks at you," he says, pointing at Mr. Allomby, "and sees the sanatorium's owner, but also the priest or lady of the evening you could have been in the outskirts of London. The number of potential Allombys is so great that, in the donor's eyes, you effectively cease to *be.*"

"Excuse me?" Mr. Allomby sputters, indignant.

"Doctor Papini is speaking figuratively," Ledesma says.

"What I'm saying is that a hypothesis can be drawn from the donor's words. Is anyone taking notes?"

He wants to make me the scribe of his effervescence. Busy my hand. Annoy me.

"The hypothesis is that we *are* because we're not everything we could be. In other words, Director Ledesma, the foundation of being is the absence of this variation, which is essentially to say that we exist in and by error."

I hear it straight from his mouth.

"Prudence, gentlemen," says Ledesma. "Let's gather our samples first, then construct our analytic framework."

"First the framework," counters Papini, "then the samples."

"I think not," says Ledesma.

"Samples," says Mr. Allomby. "And Quintana every day talks with donors, tells truth to all of them."

Me? All of them? All by myself? Gigena stands to let me pass, Menéndez opens the door, and Gurian points a finger at me.

"Let's see that magic, Quintana."


This is how I want to remember us: splayed in the grass with our pants unbuttoned, our shirts covering our bellies and our indigestion. Masters of alcohol's fumblings. Gurian removes his dentures to pick them clean of grilled meat, then stalks around on all fours in the throes of a miniature hunt until the teeth catch a beetle and return to his mouth. More wine to wash away the taste of insect. Is it bitter? Ledesma goes on reading the phrases collected during the day at the top of his lungs.

> Donor eight: "welcome"
> Donor nine: "just like I dreamed"
> Donor ten: (no record)

Donor eleven: (no record)
Donor twelve: "Our Lady of Luján"
Donor thirteen: "he doesn't love me"
Donor fourteen: "children last"
Donor fifteen: "no eyes or nose, but a mouth"
Donor sixteen: (no record)
Donor seventeen: "Denmark"

Menéndez went to bed. I hope she sleeps tight. She spent the whole day in my office, on the director's orders, watching me unfurl my candor to one donor after another. In her eyes I was a gentleman, a man of superior intelligence and ample vocabulary, a kind soul who gave toy frogs to the donors to cheer their final moments with metallic tinkling.

Of all the sensations from the day, however, I am left with the smell of lemon emanating from Papini a few yards away as he grabs the papers from Ledesma and reads on.

Donor eighteen: "touch me"
Donor nineteen: "he who sees and breathes"
Donor twenty: "Argentina wins"
Donor twenty-one: (no record)
Donor twenty-two: "life to the monster"
Donor twenty-three: "thank you"

I say, out loud, that the phrases are too short for proper analysis. I kneel in the mud and reveal my vision. Multiple devices, in a circle. Donors looking at one another. The guillotines activating sequentially, every nine seconds. Each head picking up where the last left off to make a full sentence, a paragraph. A stanza, says Gigena. A string of words worth the expense and efforts of this team.

The doctor with the mole says that carrying out my fantasy would require considerably more donors and that we'd quickly run through the nation's cancer cases. I tell him that cancer isn't the only disease an imaginary serum can cure.

Ledesma says that the idea of a circle of heads forming an articulate statement is the closest thing to happiness he can imagine. That teamwork offers an advantage because it keeps egos at bay, and that if we Argentines could agree more often, we'd be a more powerful nation. We'd deny entry to the bestial hordes from Southern Europe. We'd roll cigars in the skin of our natives. We'd impose a new kind of Christianity, grounded in the values of the Pampas and pastoral toil. Cleanse the foreign pestilence of the Brazilian blacks. Reclaim Uruguay as our natural and legitimate backyard. Cast provincial Chile into the Pacific.

He falls into a bug-eyed silence. He thanks us for casting off the shackles of good manners in the name of scientific audacity and calls for a round of applause. For me. Starting tomorrow, the entire sanatorium will dedicate itself to making my vision a reality.

The wind in my face, in our faces, cracks open a sliver of lucidity. I think about Sylvia (now less than before), about how Menéndez will be mine by right and general consensus, how the donors were going to die anyway, and that I'll need to cultivate a serious gaze, as if I were very tired, so no one can tell how easy it all was.

# 4

My name begins to spread. It settles into casual conversations, remarks about the hue of my voice, furtive insinuations among the nurses, vile comparisons among my colleagues. I am split by this prism of Quintanas, Menéndez. Take your pick.

I sense the trap inherent to love and its by-products: give up being what you want, abandon your whims, offer an ear, a shoulder, a hand; offer yourself up entirely and piecemeal to sign on the romantic line, when it's obviously impossible to love someone all the time. These concessions will be my payment when I've got you by the neck and have torn you a few new holes.

A botanical digression: Thompson Island, a small landmass in Tierra del Fuego, is the only natural habitat of comemadre, a plant with acicular leaves whose sap produces (in a leap between taxonomic kingdoms that warrants further study) microscopic animal larvae. These larvae devour the plant, leaving only tiny particles behind; the remains then spread to take root in the soil, and the process begins again.

If the larvae are extracted under laboratory conditions, the plant grows unchecked until it can no longer support its own weight and dies without reproducing.

The larvae, meanwhile, can easily survive in a liquid medium or hibernate indefinitely in the form of a black powder.

A few farmers in Tierra del Fuego have taken to planting comemadre as a measure against pests. It has been proven that rats love the taste of the plant and that they die within days of eating it, consumed from the inside out by the larvae.

This is my botanical digression. I show Ledesma the test tube containing the larvae. I won't be telling him about how I learned of the existence of comemadre, or the crude, coincidental encounter that brought it into my possession. I don't like to share the details of my life outside the sanatorium.

I lower my voice. I tell him the storage room in the basement is full. We need to find a way to empty it. The incinerator? Fire is filthy, and filth is a dead giveaway. Those are my exact words. It's more hygienic to inject these larvae into the bodies and make them disappear without a trace.

And more expensive. The acquaintance who gets them for me has substantial overhead. Ledesma hugs me. He whispers that Mr. Allomby will cover every cent. I linger in the embrace: I'll let him go when I'm good and ready.


Furious, Mauricio Albano Ruiz storms into Ledesma's office, asking why they postponed his donation. He interrupts our embrace. He demands his payment be returned immediately, in full.

The Argentine aristocracy's limited history works to its disadvantage. One battle against the royalists or a grandfather who signed the constitution can't compare to the sagas of European castles that span hundreds of years. As a result, many patrician families paradoxically renounce their history in their homeland, fixing their memories instead on distant ancestors on the other side of the ocean. Their memories are faulty: Edinburgh is not in England. They inherited a piece of furniture from the Netherlands adorned with allegorical figures and a coat of arms they don't understand, but not the byzantine manners of their forebears or an interest in falconry. They're satisfied to have a cow win a prize at the

Sociedad Rural, get bored at the Jockey Club, and fume over tardiness like common bureaucrats.

Ledesma tells him about the change of plans and the new devices being installed in the basement. But Mauricio doesn't want to see them. He paid for a singular death, not to finish the sentences of a bunch of illiterates and turn a sacred moment into something base, promiscuous.

We ask him to be patient. He threatens to break his confidentiality agreement and publish the details of the experiment in a major Buenos Aires newspaper. We explain to him that we have nothing to hide.

He starts screaming again. The uproar reaches Mr. Allomby, who steps into the office, shakes Mauricio's hand, and invites him to make his donation right then and there. His mentor, Doctor Papini, will measure his head and activate the device. I'll be in charge of transcribing his words

Ledesma grabs me by the lapel. He orders me to go with Papini, not lift a finger to help him, and ask for his letter of resignation as soon as the cut is made.

With a tug on this string, I'll open the door that leads to unemployment; with this other one, I'll close the door that leads to Menéndez. I need to show him that what just happened in Ledesma's office was a disgrace and that it was his fault for putting the entire experiment at risk over the whim of a suicidal dandy. I consider my options for giving him the news: keeping a few feet between us, wearing a smile that says "It's not as bad as it seems," keeping relatively still.

The dandy waits outside. Arranging the devices in a circle was my idea, but it was Gurian who came up with the universal lever to trigger the blades. There it is, in the middle of the room, announcing the inadequacy of my vision. Papini takes out his anthropometric insect, spreads its legs. He still doesn't know this is his last night in the sanatorium.

"The proper ape is lazy, Quintana. Do you know how many of the donors were atavistic? I needed to go back to the books to make sure I had it right. Most of them were partial, moderate, as if they'd mixed with us. You can't study a dog by applying parameters meant for a wolf."

He's tired. He's not my enemy anymore, not entirely, either because he doesn't want to be or because his love for Menéndez didn't survive the loss of a tooth and he's grateful I laid down the law. Which is why he pretends I'm listening to him.

He wants to do everything by the book. It's his first time. He tries to choose the best guillotine for Mauricio, but we don't know which is first in the sequence. Just in case, he wipes each of them down with the sleeve of his suit jacket.


"My brother Mauricio is upstairs," Mauricio says when we open the door. "Would it be all right if I invited him in?"

I ask why.

"I want him to be present," Mauricio says. "It's my dying wish."

I explain to him that dying wishes were invented to clear the consciences of next of kin or soldiers on a firing squad, but that there's no need here because everything's already squeaky clean, as befits a scientific experiment. He should say good-bye now.

"Send him my regards," says Mauricio.


After measuring him, Papini shows him to his seat and, before closing the device around him, shakes his hand vigorously.

Mauricio notices the filth on his sleeve. Papini steps back and pulls the lever.

The sequence begins with the device opposite Mauricio, who calculates with a glance how long he has left: sixty-three seconds. The sound of the second blade fills the room, right on time. The third and fourth seem to follow more quickly because their echoes overlay the others. Mauricio can feel the vibrations in his body; he turns to watch their approach.

"Please, make it stop," he says.

It's not an outrageous request. But our consternation lasts until the next blade. We're being asked to discard—in fourteen seconds, thirteen—our professionalism in favor of a gauchada. Terrible way to describe a good deed. It likens my generosity to that of some lousy, manure-caked gaucho who throws salt over his shoulder to ward off bad luck. I tell Mauricio it won't be possible.

I offer to walk Papini out. I wish he'd been a bit more assertive about his dismissal, fighting with Ledesma or dragging Menéndez across the floor, forcing her to dirty her smock, to flail around, fists and knees futilely thrashing, so I could stage my heroic intervention. He already said good-bye to Gurian, who wished him a bright future at some other sanatorium, and Gigena, who advised him to stay on his toes. He didn't ask for Menéndez and probably didn't run into her in the hall way on his way out. Bad luck. Just like his first and final head: no record.

I give him a firm handshake when we reach the door. He looks down at the metal frog I've left in his palm.

"We had a good run, didn't we, Quintana?" he asks without taking his eyes off the frog.

I say yes. I see no reason not to.

Today the ants spill out of the crack without forming a shape; they spread across the wall like the insects they are.

The bodies in storage are ash. Mr. Allomby holds me by the jacket so I can peer down the hole without risk of falling while I devise four or five ways to turn the tables. Benevolently, though. I'm in excellent spirits.

In two days we'll begin the sequential decapitations. Gurian and Gigena expect the results to be more like poetry than prose, given the predictably fragmentary nature of the state-ments. A fortune-teller's opacity: ethereal nouns, verbs with no easily identifiable subjects. Most of the donors have a hundred-word vocabulary, including articles and prepositions. Under these conditions, it would be hard not to lapse into poetry. At least, Ledesma says, we won't run into too much irony, which complicates interpretation. Gigena purses his lips and, after a little "hmm" that softens his disagreement, says that irony is not the exclusive purview of the educated, and that it can be seen outside small-town corner stores in the form of insult-ing nicknames. Oinking, for example, at a slim young woman.

Whatever words the heads might have uttered, whatever piece-meal sentences that were to reveal another world, or our own, will remain unknown.

The groundskeeper's shed catches fire a third time. The wind sends the blaze climbing up the nearest trees. One of the flam-ing branches breaks off, sails toward the entrance, and lands on a pile of papers. General stupidity reigns long enough to allow the flames from the burning pile of papers to lap at the wood paneling and then spread across it in a single burst, encircling the door to the men's bathroom, with Mr. Allomby inside. We believe the fire can be controlled. The only fear is Mr. Allomby's, and it's getting louder. He's screaming like an animal. I don't know what kind. Just an animal. He's pounding so hard on the door it's about to break. His hands must be bleeding.

Ledesma stops to think. Considers what orders to give. Gigena walks toward the flames and tries the doorknob. He burns over the perfection of his old scars.

Those of us who do nothing (let maintenance take care of it, says Gurian) watch Mr. Allomby emerge with clumps of hair between his fingers, smoldering eyebrows, and hands covered in a liquid streaming down his arms from inside his jacket.

Menéndez appears with a bucket of water. She debates whether to douse Mr. Allomby, relieving his pain, or the wall, preventing the fire from spreading to the rest of the sanatorium.

Too indecisive for a head nurse. I notice that the hot bricks above Mr. Allomby are about to fall. I jump toward him and grab his legs, pulling him back and winning the admiration of all present, who can sense my bravery among the screams and the smoke.

Menéndez's water hits the floor, late. It does not relieve Mr. Allomby's pain or prevent the fire from consuming the rest of the building, but it does cause Ledesma to slip, land face-first on the floor, and vanish from sight.

Before long, civility is as scant as breathable air. One patient tears the intravenous drip from his arm and knocks over its metal stand to block anyone who might catch up to him as he sprints for the exit. Gurian takes every shortcut on his way out, a detached look on his face.

I use the blazing wall to light a cigarette: as studied gestures go, it is by far the best I've ever made. I dedicate it to no one but myself. Menéndez is on her haunches, very pale. She can't see me through the smoke. I call her by her first name, waving the cigarette back and forth. Its red ember is the only thing she can make out.

She calls me "Doctor" and lets herself be guided by my voice until I take her by the arm, and then by the neck. I lean her forward, tell her to bend her knees. She needs to walk faster. To breathe. To see me in profile and wonder why it took her so long to let herself be found. To stumble over her own feet. To stop trying to hide her surrender.

I drag her outside, into the fields, into the countryside that surrounds the sanatorium. Her shoes are covered in mud, her apron, too. Why not her face? I push it into the mud to cool her off. I drag her further and further from the sanatorium. For her own good, and so no one can see.

We're far away now. Now her neck bears the marks of my fingers. She can breathe the night air. Like all nurses, she believes air is different at night than it is during the day. She is a grateful woman.

I show her that my shoes have come untied. I can't walk any further: I might trip over them and fall. With her indestructible love and her skinned knees on the ground, Menéndez reaches for the strings.

| 2009 | *Buenos Aires* |

I'm reading the draft of a doctoral dissertation on my life and the things I've done. Its author is one Ms. Lynda Carter of Yale University. Lynda informs me in her cover letter that she was born and educated in Baltimore, that she went to fat camp when she was fifteen, and that a patriotic shiver runs through her whenever she hears a song that mentions apple pie. Sharing her name with the star of *Wonder Woman* makes her feel dirty, too pop culture. She wants to change it so she can stop feeling like her life's being broadcast from the seventies. "I'm a martyr of homonymy," she writes.

What follows is her synopsis of me: I have a hand with four fingers; I lost the fifth. I have a body, which is my own, and a nonstandard head that cost me a lot of money. A museum in Copenhagen offered double that sum to cover me with plastic and put me on display when I die. Two Danish human rights organizations are suing the museum for promoting "a concept of the body as merchandise." A lesbian collective had a sit-in at the entrance to the museum in solidarity with my right to put a price on my body, as is done with any art object.

These, according to Ms. Carter, are the threads that make up the fabric of me, my corset, the frame against which my silhouette takes shape. Those are the words she uses. She also says that my contribution to the field of art is remarkably consistent, and that she wouldn't be surprised if my last name started being used as an adjective in the medium term. She presents this as common sense, with numbers: websites, visitors to the Milan retrospective, sales figures.

She dedicates eight chapters to my collaborations with Lucio Lavat—more than two-thirds of the text. The final quotation is from a cruel, ridiculous article published recently in the *New York Times,* in which Lavat is described as an older version of me "with no direction or future in the art market." Offended, Lynda writes five pages vindicating him, with truth and love on her side.

I'm suddenly curious to see a recent picture of Lucio. I look online, but the first few pages of search results yield only the same photos from two or three years ago and a few graphics and canvases from his recent gallery shows. (It seems he went back to framed paintings.) I find what I'm looking for on Lynda Carter's personal webpage, in photos from her last birthday that show Lucio giving her a hug, wearing a party hat and his current face. We still look remarkably alike.

The dissertation is bound in faux leather. I pause to inspect it before reading on. The text is austere in tone except for the first footnote, in which Lynda passionately argues that I orchestrated my life from the start without a single misstep, and that it—my work, me—represents the culmination (or the end, it isn't entirely clear) of the project of the historical avant-garde. I soon discover that all the footnotes in Lynda's dissertation are equally harebrained. According to her academic whim, I am "an artist of the binary," the "offspring of capitalist culture," the salvation of art and its living negation.

The study doesn't end up in the trash because of an envelope on its back cover, which contains a handwritten letter from Lucio Lavat asking me not to throw it out, to instead consider helping Lynda in any way I can.

It must have been arduous to write such a long letter by hand.

# 2

Dear Lynda: in chapter two, you say my adolescence was "in keeping with the customs of a middle-class family in Buenos Aires, complete with piano instructors and TV viewing restrictions." The acuity of the phrase is impressive—it demonstrates your knowledge of the social and cultural panorama of Argentina during those years, which must have cost you hours of mind-numbing calculations. The allusions to soccer and tango, on the other hand, detract from the rest of the chapter. They should be removed.

Below, you'll find some additional information.

As if I have the words KICK ME stamped across my forehead in a Soviet-era font, I turn sixteen with a head full of curls and a body weighing two hundred and sixty-five pounds, one hundred and fifty of which are my true self (at that age, one believes that sort of thing), wrapped in a hundred and fifteen of pure fat. I have a belly that I rest on my knees to avoid falling forward when I sit, and breasts that would be lovely on a normal-sized girl if it weren't for the little tufts of hair starting to sprout between them. I'm a man, but first and foremost I'm an appalling fatso.

If the world shames me, if even the most vulgar creatures look good next to me, it's without my consent. Other fatsos traffic in affection and adopt despicable attitudes: they know how to listen to problems, help with exams, grab afternoon snacks with the girls. I reject and am rejected in turn, without even trying. I talk to no one, am poised to come in last in the sprint out of virginity, and don't wear t-shirts with logos on them. If someone compares me to a suckling pig, a cow, or a whale, I raise an eyebrow à la Bette Davis and leave my face like that until whoever it is understands: Nothing they say could offend me. Ever.

Mom and Dad unknowingly underwrite my girth. My day begins with an act of domestic larceny that buys me the two alfajores I eat on my walk to school, a chicken cutlet on a roll with mayonnaise during recess, plus a dozen empanadas and three slices of pizza on my way home, which I eat in different pizzerias to avoid drawing attention to myself. All this passes my lips before lunch, which I eat at home. The volume increases at night. Before bed, I lock myself in the bathroom under the pretense of masturbation, which Mom and Dad respect, and polish off a one-pound tub of dulce de leche. This is how I develop a phobia of being asphyxiated by my own jowls in the night and begin to sleep fitfully, certain I'm alone in this fear.

I keep pets in my desk drawer. The hamster they bought me when I was six, which only lasted two days, floats in a jar of formaldehyde. Sometimes I give it a nudge with my pencil and watch it spin. Then there's Wright, the desiccated turtle that the family left out on the balcony under the unrelenting sun. I peer into his box every now and then. His death might just be a lethargic state he recovers from one day, demanding lettuce. (I still have him. Lucio used to joke about showing him at the Guggenheim.) I also have two live parakeets that pop out and perch on my hand whenever I open the drawer. Those are going in the garbage when they die, because a hamster and a turtle are nice souvenirs, but four corpses make a cemetery, and we all have our limits.

Before I turn eighteen, I get sick and am confined to bed. I see it as a chance to develop some semblance of a social life:

I imagine the pounds melting off me from the fever and a circle of classmates standing around me, rooting for my recovery. This is not what happens. I'm diagnosed with measles, a highly contagious and unfairly infantile disease. No one comes to visit. Mom and Dad seize the opportunity to love me without pause.

By the time I finish treatment, I'm a whole other person: just as fat, but less fascinated by solitude. I stamp the words LOOK AT ME in tiny letters across my forehead, hoping someone might come in close to read them, close enough for me to steal a kiss. I tell my classmates that having fatso boobs deforms your nipples and show them what I mean; I compete with the girls at school over who has the longest eyelashes and correct the uninformed at the top of my lungs.

The result is a monolithic solitude and an internal monologue that remains uninterrupted until the day another voice—which is mine, but distilled—tells me that sooner or later I'll need to give life to the monster.

At that age, my dear Lynda Carter, the superficial struggle of "me against the world" was the first step on a slippery slope to "me against myself." Fixing this, becoming a friend or accomplice to myself, would set me apart (or so I believed) from the rest of the species. I wanted to be a man without contradictions whose unshakeable balance revealed the inner strife of those around him. But my fat, my aforementioned solitude, and my desire to take part in love came between me and the constancy I was after.

I tackle the fat skeptically, with diets that last roughly a week, or until I throw in the towel and eat a whole pizza in one sitting. My solitude feels directly connected to my weight. My notion of love is a series of snapshots or jump cuts: I can imagine a first kiss, five minutes of a vacation, an argument easily won—but not the continuity, the boredom, or what to do with the same person, day after day.

Who could find me attractive, break me in? Who might want to explore the world of obesity with me? And where? School isn't an option, neither are bars or clubs, and I don't get invited to parties. I observe the teenage social scene from a seat in the very last row. How does it work? The television offers no examples, except in comedies. I can't imitate my classmates' tactics: those only work in the market of the physically acceptable. I don't want to try out my moves on someone with a short temper and end up facedown in a ditch. Is there a way to hit on someone that doesn't involve professing or confessing?

This is what I hear: "If you want sex, you have to show you're available." So simple, so practical. What available persona can I invent for myself? TOUCH ME, the new writing on my forehead entreats—followed, in smaller letters, by PLEASE. I'm primed to have sex with the whole country, and I suspect this makes the whole country a little queasy. What other option is there but to pay for it? I shut myself in the bathroom with the classified ads from *Clarín,* a pencil, and my dulce de leche; two hours later, I'm trembling in the doorway of a building in Recoleta with fifty pesos in my hand. The ad announced services "starting at twenty pesos," but I want them to fake it with conviction.

I step into an apartment with leatherette sofas. A man with gray hair invites me to sit, inspects me in silence, and offers me my first cigarette ever, which I don't smoke. He asks me for the money and returns the thirty extra pesos, patting me on the shoulder. "Take your pick." He opens a door.

Before my options appear, I wonder what my selection crite-
ria should be, what preferences I'm expected to have. When
they finally walk out, though, I stop thinking entirely—my
arousal paralyzes me, turns me into a primate. They're four
gorgeous men, all legs and pectorals, and I'm one of those
clients who make an escort question their life choices. Disgust
immediately spreads across three of their faces. Momentarily
taken aback by this, I have time to observe the fourth: he is
skinny and hunched, and, contrary to expectations, seems
eager—at a distance from the others, he steps toward me. His
name is Sebastian. With him comes the memory of an old
family photo.

Someone says, "Photo!" I'm there, five years old. Everyone
clamors to stand around some meaningful object, a cake,
anticipating the best spots in the image's composition and
the family hierarchy. It matters whether you stand next
to Grandpa or out on the edge, surrounded by second-rate
cousins or near the one who smells bad. The family's elders
form the axis of the photo, followed by a circle of parents
who act like they have more money than they do, then one
of direct descendants and their newborns, with particular
visual emphasis on the babies. Next comes the circle of less-
dedicated offspring, the ones who bring home bad grades or
get seduced by taxi drivers, then comes the circle of aunts
and uncles, then the one of in-laws. Finally, all the way at the
edge, the circle of new girlfriends, boyfriends, and that one
friend someone invited. They raise their glasses. It's a historic
photo of the whole family, historic because the whole family's
there. Copies must be requested and distributed: the in-laws
take care of that. They go to pick up the prints and open the
envelope. They expect to find a few questionable hairstyles,

but not a neighbor who knows only the party's hosts and has only ever spoken to them across the fence that divides their lots. But there she is, right there next to Grandpa, a perfect stranger in dark sunglasses raising her glass highest of all.

Sebastian is like the neighbor in that photo, something between a stain and an unwitting terrorist, as he stands there with the three other men offering themselves to my gaze. It's not his sickly coloring that makes me choose him, or his small frame, or his bowed legs—it's the desire I hadn't expected to see in his eyes.

The room is at the end of a hallway. Sebastian hangs off me with his hand in my pants, rubbing himself against me so sloppily, so chaotically, that I feel like I'm the one who should be giving him lessons. This is sex, see? That goes here, try not to breathe when you do this, save that until the very end. I make a decision: to behave from now on (in the life that starts now) as if I know it all. By the time I open the door, I already feel like an expert.

When we finish, Sebastian—his skin surprisingly green for a human being and one knee scraped bright red by the floor—tells me he'd been waiting (he's a romantic) for his dream client to walk through the door, the one he'd been searching for among all the others, and that his dream client is me. He wants us to be together: the way I look, there's no way I'd ever cheat on him. He assumes I'll fall in love with him within two or three days. He apologizes for having to charge me and offers me my second cigarette ever, which I smoke as he digs around in his bag.

He turns to me with his fists held out and asks me to choose one. I'm in my new phase of knowing it all, so I choose both. He opens his hands to show me his gift: in each is a slightly rusted metal frog no bigger than a nut. If you press their back legs down with one finger, they spring up in the air and a little bell inside them rings; the high-pitched noise continues when they return to the ground, making them easier to find. Sebastian says they're toys for blind children.

His grandfather César has given them to him, hoping he'll keep them as relics. The idea of a relic is somewhat confusing for an eight-year-old. Sebastian smells a rat. He suspects his family of concealing a hereditary condition that will leave him blind before long. Or that they wish he were blind: maybe the frogs are designed to steal his light.

He tells no one about this. He believes he can protect himself from the disease by staying away from the frogs and using his eyes as little as possible. He avoids windows. When he goes outside, he makes a visor of his hands. His grandfather César notices the change and suggests he be taken to an optometrist. Once there, he keeps his eyes shut, afraid the doctor's flashlight will pierce them. He cannot be convinced otherwise and is diagnosed with photophobia.

Now it's his family that forbids him from going near windows. He feels more loved and cared for than before. Unused, Sebastian's eyes and the metal frogs become relics.

I return home with a new awareness of sex and a strong desire to have more of it. I slip my gift into my desk and discover that mechanical objects, at rest, frighten the parakeets.

We get together at night, in his apartment. Sebastian avoids going out during the day, but when he does, he always wears dark glasses. He lives in an office building from the seventies with doors that stay open until late in the evening, fluorescent lighting—the only kind that doesn't hurt him—and a

Formica reception desk manned by a world-weary old-timer who smokes with his head resting against a plush directory board where the names of businesses are spelled out in Bakelite.

Sebastian isn't interested in high culture. To his mind, it isn't particularly elevated, or it's elevated by a pair of stilettos. He has a noncommittal adjective for everything I show him, and my enthusiasm for initiating him into my world is dampened until some object more to his taste, something figurative, makes him smile.

I invite him to my parents' house and introduce him as a friend; in a momentary lapse of judgment, we lock ourselves in the bathroom. My parents say nothing about the episode, but Mom interrupts breakfast a week later, pointing a finger at me.

"I know what you do in there, with your dulce de leche."

The best advice I can offer, Lynda, for having a nice dinner with friends, is to avoid any reference to how much your relationship with your working-class lover, the one you met a week earlier in an unmentionable place, has changed the way you see the world. There's no need for it.

I fall in love with Sebastian in three days, just as he predicted, but love turns my head as soft as an old lady's slipper, and I demand that he quit his job and find something more hygienic. I tell him that monogamy, like all artificial things, is absolutely necessary because man invents only what he needs. My aphorism leaves him speechless.

He's with me because he believes I could never cheat on him, but he doesn't love me (he repeats: he doesn't love me) because I'm capable of saying things like what I just said. He's terribly sad. If I don't accept the asymmetries of the relationship, if I try to recalibrate them, we're through. I yield to his threat. But while I keep my mouth shut and speculate on his changing, he's already anticipating the day when I fall out of love.

Every couple of days we have a cigarette down in the building's lobby, listening to the ancient receptionist talk about the future with little creativity and even less interest. I give Sebastian a drawing of the man's ear. He could have eventually sold it for a good price, but he's disorganized and loses it, along with the portraits I do of him when I go back to being a genius, or half of one, just for him.

In her dissertation, Lynda Carter uses comparison tables and data about cranial mass to explain the minutiae of my genius.

I hand Mom the teacher's note. *Dear Mrs. Mom, please be so kind as to come in for a conversation about your son's behavior.* My behavior, according to the standard parameters for six-year-old children, is very good. I'm a delight. Women pinch my cheeks.

Mom goes to the meeting ready to raise hell. She brings me with her so I can see how much she loves me. My teacher is direct: she accuses my mother of doing my drawing homework. A very loving gesture, she explains, but also an invitation to laziness. But Mom never does my homework, ever. We need to clear up the misunderstanding.

My teacher opens her desk drawer and takes out my notebook. She says that children my age draw a certain way: simple, one-dimensional pictures marked by exaggeration and arbitrary lines. She is convinced she's caught us in a lie, and she underscores this after her little speech by pulling a face that says "give up" as she opens my notebook and holds up my latest drawing. It's a hand, done in pencil.

Now Mom is on my teacher's side and the two of them wait, in sisterly silence, for an explanation. I don't understand. I ask them why they don't like it. Mom gets flustered. My teacher asks, "Who drew that for you?" I ask for a pencil and within three minutes have repeated the drawing on another sheet of paper.

The child prodigy is a repulsive creature. It can be measured according to the degree of its anomaly, the fence around its isolation: its so-called talent.

They let me keep the electrodes after each round of tests. I collect them, setting one on top of another in a corner of my room until they form a tall stack. Around the same time I realize how useless, boring, and stupidly tragic the situation is, the specialists determine that the right hemisphere of my brain is more active than the left and that I have exceptionally developed visual-spatial perception, hence my talent for drawing.

A specialist in a Lacoste shirt says, "The best thing for you, kid, will be learning not to mix the wheat up with the chaff. Real geniuses aren't pedantic. No playing tricks on your classmates or embarrassing your teachers. Remember, only half of you is a genius—the right half. Keep the left half humble."

Aside from this clearly demarcated perfection and some talent for written and oral expression, my persona is rather plebeian: I have trouble with math and staying focused. Over the course of three months, I am asked to draw hands, cylinders (I make them transparent, to show off the ant I trap inside), and the complete musculature of the human body, which I infer through the skin. There's something covert about the tests; my teacher, the principal, and my parents shroud them in silence. I don't think a six-year-old is prepared for a silence like that. I'm certainly not.

I don't understand what's going on in my head and think I might have a tumor. The specialists ask me to draw it. This is what I make: my face, with an open door in the middle of my forehead. Behind the door is a brain made of hexagonal cells, like a honeycomb, with a bee feeding its larvae in each. "Why did you draw yourself smiling?" they ask. I'm not the one smiling, I explain, it's the cancer. I point out that they haven't seen the whole drawing yet. If you hold the paper up to the light, the recto and verso form a single image. On the back I've drawn a cross section of the face with the cerebral beehive exposed in full: with their tiny legs, two bees turn a set of minuscule pulleys connected to the corners of my mouth by a cord. With that cord, they hoist my smile.

I need to be made useful. The school principal thinks it would be best to present me to the public on prime-time news. The specialists think the idea is completely ridiculous, unless of course my parents want to turn me into a circus monkey and really screw up my head. Instead, they propose taking me on tour to do more intensive studies with the help of an "international team of scientists." Mom is in favor of this option if that's what I want, a position Dad considers too democratic. He thinks we should combine the proposals and have a news program follow the tour, which he says will open doors for me; a decision like that can't be left to a six-year-old kid.

Silvio Soldán interviews me before my first "international" session. He calls me a "shining young example for the New Argentina." Mom, Dad, and the specialists make gestures at me from behind the cameras, but Soldán is kneeling at my level and I can barely see them; blurry like that, they're a sample of the average Argentinean family watching me live on Channel Nine. I think, no one likes a child prodigy in a Dior vest.

In the fourth session, they pit me against an autistic boy from Canada who does what I do but with a vacant look in his eyes and more snot. His talent glows brighter against this back-drop of idiocy. He jerks around like he's trying to shake off canary feathers and can reproduce anything that's put in front of him with photographic precision.

They have us sit on stage, one behind the other, facing Mantegna's famous *Lamentation of Christ*. They explain to me that I'm supposed to look over the other boy's shoulder and draw exactly what he draws; since he never makes mis-takes (it's been proven, they say), the hope is that my copy of his copy will be just as perfect in perspective and detail as the original, without adulteration.

The specialist in the Lacoste shirt pulls me to the side and says, "When you realize you can't handle a situation, kid, you'll go from zero to sixty, from white to black, from stupid to feeling as lucid as if you'd just done a line of cocaine. When that happens, try to find a middle ground."

Of all my options for defeating the Canadian, the sexual one stands out. Ten minutes later, I get the chance I've been wait-ing for. The boy wants to use the toilet. They can tell because he has his hand in his pants and is rubbing himself furiously. I offer to take him.

The man in the Lacoste shirt says, "Be careful with him, kid. Open the door for him, wait for him to take a piss, wash and dry his hands, and walk him back. We'd appreciate it."

I walk the boy to the bathroom, close myself in with him, and make him lower his pants. Then I hold his head against the wall with one hand as I stick a finger up his ass. When he returns to the stage, he's a different child: a little less autistic and a lot less talented. His Christ deteriorates from the waist down, one weak stroke after another; by the time he gets to the feet, his drawing is completely inadmissible—in other words, like something a normal child would produce. They let him finish, and he's taken away by his parents. The specialists put my drawing, the Canadian's drawing, and the Mantegna on a podium. Soldán turns to the camera and says, "Argentina wins."

We say good-bye to the specialists and the cameras before we leave. Dad wants to frame my copy of the Mantegna. Mom doesn't, and she offers solid arguments: it wouldn't go with the rest of our pictures, and we're not religious. The dispute is resolved by the news that my drawing has disappeared from the podium. No one sees it again until I meet Lucio Lavat.

At first I find the thought of being a prodigy seductive. Later, in a straightforward and age appropriate way, I understand there's no such thing as a lasting prodigy. How long does it take a miracle, a Biblical plague, to become routine? How much manna? Children last, but not child prodigies. My drawings become increasingly intricate and predictable. The first to go is Soldán, because there's no arc to the story. Am I suddenly going to start drawing better? Am I going to lose my mind? No. He says good-bye over the phone, thanks me, and wishes me a bright future. There's no turning back for the specialists; I'm like a child forced into piano lessons. We slide into boredom together.

The electrodes are back on my head, thorax, and hands. It's cold on the stage (it's just a platform, but it feels huge to me), and I'm embarrassed to be up there half-naked. The man in the Lacoste shirt says, "This is the last time we'll do this, kid. Think of it as the crowning moment of our attempt to insert you into a society that doesn't tolerate difference."

An invitation to enroll in a program for gifted youth arrives from Canada, but it's only a partial scholarship. An agency offers me a reasonable sum to illustrate an advertisement for electric razors, and Dad turns them down. He leans forward and says, "It's time for you to start acting like a normal boy again, don't you think?" I change schools the following year. "If you don't mention any of this, you'll make lots of friends," says Mom. They're not big on subtlety.

The man in the Lacoste shirt comes to visit. "You've had some pretty amazing experiences, kid. But you still haven't had the most amazing one of all: a happy childhood. Over time you'll turn into a regular little boy, you'll see. Everyone's got their minds on their own asses, and it might get annoying if yours seems cleaner. Follow?"

There is, apparently, a direct correlation between sadness and calcium loss. Most children aren't aware of the connection, but if they give in to the darkness, it'll leave their mouths empty. Their teeth loosen and their gums recede until a presumably innocuous bite into a peach leaves them with a gap and they stop smiling, and then the sadness builds, and it's all downhill from there. My baby teeth fall out all at once, and it takes years for my permanent teeth to come in. They make me purees. Baby food. My bones grow fragile: if someone touches me, I turn to dust. I forget what a sandwich is. Personhood is being able to chew; while I wait for my turn to be a person, they send me to piano lessons, but I'm entirely mediocre. Maybe I'm using the wrong half.

They give me pills to stimulate my appetite. My permanent teeth come in, breaking through my gums. I get fat from the inside out. For the first few months, the fat settles unevenly: I'm pitiful from the knees down and a pig from the knees up. But I can chew.

I keep eating, and by the time I'm eighteen there's enough room in me for four people and for the monster I plan to make, but not for being in love. That old, sturdy piece of furniture won't fit through the door.

Sebastian takes the story of my childhood lightly: I'm selling a tragedy, but he buys a vaudeville. He can't stop laughing. I tell the story twice, but his reaction doesn't change.

My parents give me a trip to Mendoza as a gift, and as an opportunity to think about my academic future at a summery pace. I increase the modest spending money they provide by 40 percent with funds stolen directly from their wallets on three separate occasions. As a result, the maid is nearly fired. I invite Sebastian along to see the sights and sample more rural modes of prostitution.

People with long fingers touch things as if they were leaving a trail of slime on them. Sebastian, too. When he sees in my face that I still love him, he softly pushes me away with fingers like that. It happens two or three times during the trip. He likes the first place we see, a two star hotel. Before falling asleep, he asks me never to get rid of the metal frogs. The next day he wakes me with the news that we've signed up for a bicycle race.

Sebastian is at the five-hundred-meter mark and is taking a curve. I've made it one hundred meters. I'm comforted by the fact that he can't see my failure, the way I have to extract the bike from my ass.

I spend a while observing the kind of people who attend these events. Their clothes. The faces of the ones who've bet that I'll be the first to give up.

The winning cyclists cross the finish line. There are the girls hanging from their necks and the mothers, but the really moving scenes arrive with the moral victors, the ones who wanted to have a positive experience, defying their age or the loss of a leg. Sebastian isn't among them: he doesn't reach the finish line, or return to the hotel.

I take a bus back to Buenos Aires ahead of schedule, without telling anyone. The receptionist is listening to the replay of a soccer game on a run-down radio and hands over the keys without looking at me. The electricity in Sebastian's apartment has been shut off. There's barely anything of his there— a few shirts.

I wait there for ten days, until the end of my vacation. I return the keys to the receptionist and go back to my parents, who aren't surprised by my lack of a tan or my lies about having a lovely time, but are discreet about it.

I go back a couple times to ask about him, but there's no news. The last time, the receptionist points to the plush directory board: the apartment is now a weight-loss center.

Between the sadness of going back to that place and the burden of nostalgia, I can conceive of the discipline required for a diet. I ask my parents for the money and bring them electronic printouts from the scale, logging each pound I lose. The first forty-five come off in three months. Teenagers' bodies are reliable that way: their skin is still elastic, and their liver and kidneys aren't ruined yet, so all it takes is a systematic and sustained change of diet to clear up their acne and perk up their breasts. Add in a few trips to the gym, and the possibility of a torso even begins to emerge.

I enroll in fine arts to learn technical vocabulary, get a sense of the market, and give myself a few easy wins. When I lose another fifteen pounds, my classmates recognize me as that sort-of child prodigy from television and suddenly understand why I ace my classes and dazzle my professors so easily. They approach me, trying to figure out what I can do for them, and eventually find me—a hundred pounds lighter now—attractive.

In those days, Lynda, I believed each of my fingers represented a quantifiable amount of me.

# 3

You should remove the phrase "seed of his future talent" and the eight pages about the scandal with Damien Hirst. They're awkward, both for me personally and for the dissertation.

A Big Mac doesn't taste the same in Beijing as it does in Toronto or Lisbon, but travelers believe in a universal flavor that takes them home in a single bite: they eat McDonald's name-first. That's what I want for myself. At twenty-two, on a government fellowship to study art, I realize that the doors my father was talking about aren't found in minor galleries or by word of mouth; they aren't in competitions or fellowships: they're in having a name. My plan is to stamp mine on the forehead of a mainstream audience overlooked by the art world, to make it grow inward from the margin until it reaches the real consumers at their doorsteps. Everyone debates the ethics of images: matrons clucking over the crassness of the latest ass on the cover of some magazine, sports fans scrutinizing the photo of a foul to justify a free kick, children cracking open a medical textbook in search of deformities. My first piece needs to make people cringe, to be in poor taste. A Nazi or anti-Nazi performance in which an actual Jew is beaten. The genital mutilation of an African woman projected in an infinite loop on the façade of a public hospital.

That soft voice, more lucid than my own, tells me the time has come to give life to the monster.

They tell me about him over dinner one night. All the necessary elements are there: he is a petite child, lovely, with two heads. The first grows normally, from his neck. The second hangs languid behind: it has no eyes or nose, but it does have a mouth—small and well formed, with premature teeth. It can't be removed because the two heads share a brain, or because the boy has two brains, or because he is two boys. No one knows for sure.

His mother, cowardly or prescient, died in childbirth. That was two weeks ago, and the child oozes health. His father shows him off on news programs and morning shows as irrefutable proof of God's love. Someone adds that children are tying their heads together in schoolyards across the country and explains the rules of the game to me.

This, sweet happiness, is my monster. In the middle of a media frenzy. I call the father and say I'm going to dedicate my first show to the three of them. I don't offer money. I use the terms "art" and "social acceptance" in the same sentence, and the good man remembers me from my days on television. He and the child are at my disposal.

Parents, Lynda, tend to burden their children with such weighty expectations. This man wanted his to be two people. As I'm sure you know, his dream came true a few years ago, when the lone mouth began to speak with unexpected intelligence. It's strange that you didn't include this detail in your study. I'll send you the transcript.

I find an exhibition space before attention shifts to other monsters. The gallerist makes room for the television cameras. The audience consists partially of members of the working class who want to see the two-headed baby in person and partially of the same old crowd, charmed by the novelty of attending a show with the first group. Grade-school teachers, prime-time heartthrobs, the wives of entrepreneurs, and artisans from the Plaza Francia, united to bring me a measure of worldly success, crowd together in front of the glass that separates them from my piece.

On the far side of the room, the father lies facedown on a bed. His son sleeps beside him. Their heads are joined exactly where the baby's second head should be, as if it had been removed and replaced with the father's. The bed splits in two, and the father's body slips down into the divide until only his head, attached to his son's, remains.

It's a simple trick: the baby is knocked out with cooking gas and its second head is covered by a silicone reproduction of the father's face and body. Lynda Carter either forgets to mention this or doesn't know how it was done, but she does point out, brandishing her discovery, that original tapes from the event recently fetched an interesting sum at Sotheby's. She also says that "in this displacement of the senses, the cephalic union of father and son can be read as a gesture toward the umbilical cord."

The photographer stands me between the father and the baby. The father and the baby look straight ahead; I'm looking to the left of the frame, at an argument between journalists and the public about inappropriate use of the baby, crossing lines, and compassion or the lack thereof. The argument quickly turns personal: someone wants to kick my ass. This shoots me from a single column in the culture section to a half-page spread in lifestyle.

I study their faces one by one, calculating the scandal. Until I see my own. Silence. Several people think Lucio Lavat's entrance is part of the piece. We're the same: same height, same nose, same teeth. Our heads are even the same shape, and we don't have a single drop of blood in common.

Lucio has been talking since we first caught sight of each other, but I only just started listening to him: he's making a clever remark about failure. I'm confused. Maybe I was the one who brought it up. Simultaneously, or perhaps a moment earlier, a woman in the audience wearing green gloves clenches her jaw and looks me in the eye when Lucio says "failure" in that crystalline voice of his.

Lucio said in a recent interview that seeing his reflection in me stirred no new feelings because my face isn't novel to him. This was said for effect; I don't believe him. You should tell him so, Lynda.

The idea of sleeping with Lucio drives me wild. I can't tell what he thinks; I have a hard time reading him. I see him as an action figure of me with better legs and an out-of-sync voice. Maybe he's uncomfortable. After the show, he invites me to his place. I skip the obligatory dinner with the baby's father and the gallerist to go with him.

He lives in a building from the fifties with semicircular balconies. We end up in the same elevator as the woman with the green gloves from the gallery. She congratulates me on the show. Lucio, silent, bows his head.

He opens the door onto a generous, square living room, there's a three-foot mound of something that at first glance looks like fat or brown gelatin. "We're in the same line of work," he says. I don't understand right away. He's telling me that he is, or wants to be, an artist. It seems unreal. Do we have the same fingerprints, too? The same morning breath?

There's a bad smell, a pile of bones with bits of flesh still on them, and two pots brimming with more bones. He says he boils them for the gelatin, to use in soft sculptures, but that he hasn't hit on the right consistency yet. His pieces melt in the living room. I make my own clever remark about failure. Then I bring up the topic of our physical resemblance. How strange it is that our paths never crossed before. Lucio says he's known me for years.

I demand proof. He points to a framed copy, in charcoal, of Mantegna's Christ.

His mother compares him to me, stands him next to the television screen. Lucio is eight, two years older than me, but besides that, we're the same. During my brief childhood stardom, he is an attraction among his neighbors and classmates.

Hoping to take a photo of the two of us, his mother brings him to see me square off against the autistic Canadian. Lucio hides in the crowd. The idea of meeting me terrifies him.

The man in the Lacoste shirt picks him up (Lucio doesn't remember, but it must have been him), scolds him for his carelessness, and hands him my copy of the Mantegna. Lucio doesn't clear up the misunderstanding. He watches me leave with my parents.

He thinks of us as two points connected by a line of solid matter. He doesn't know how long this line is, but he believes the moment will come when it can't stretch any further and one of us will drop to the ground.

He gives his mother the drawing as an apology for ruining the encounter she'd planned, but she doesn't speak to him for a week. Eventually she gives in and signs him up for art classes.

It only takes him a few months to become an expert. He copies my copy of the Mantegna with incredible accuracy.

He shows it to no one. He's at a disadvantage: he's competing with a six-year-old. His talent blossoms under this repression, and it gets him a grant to continue his studies in Italy by the time he's twelve.

Having several museums a stone's throw from the classroom doesn't save him from being taught with slides and textbook reproductions. As a student, he worships Velázquez and adores Hogarth. Midsemester, after a particularly blurry week in the thick of things, he runs away to London. They find him two months later, trying to steal an Aubrey Beardsley (and almost succeeding).

He becomes hot news in England. A big-time journalist writes a column on the case in which he laments the many childhoods destroyed by the war in the "Falklands," wonders whether public education receives sufficient funding, makes a joke about the queen, talks about peace, and concludes with a plea on behalf of Lucio, "a twelve-year-old boy who crosses international lines for real art."

The museum, in all its paternalism (it is an English museum), publicly pardons Lucio for his attempted robbery. An arts institute in Oslo goes one step further, offering him a fellowship to study there for two years. Lucio and his mother move to Oslo with housing and a stipend courtesy of the state.

Against a backdrop of Norwegians, Lucio's mother calls his father's architecture firm in Buenos Aires and informs him that he can start divorce proceedings, then moves herself and her son in with a guy named Dag.

Dag introduces Lucio to Norway's formidable language. He teaches history at the university five months of the year and is just settling into his seven months of self-satisfaction and marijuana. He finds Lucio's attempted theft of the Beardsley admirable and complains about what he describes as the "indecisive nature" of his countrymen.

Lucio's father travels to Norway and serves as the witness at his ex-wife's wedding to Dag. While the couple is off on their honeymoon, father and son make up for lost time watching vhs tapes of hours and hours of Argentinean television. Lucio searches for news about me. My absence makes him uncomfortable.

When he turns eighteen, he goes back to Buenos Aires to formalize his studies abroad. If his father buys him an apartment and promises him the funds to visit his mother once a year, Lucio is inclined not to do anything of significance until he's twenty-three. To his father, this seems like a good deal.

Lucio travels a lot. He is perpetually lovely and thin, and amasses a collection of accessories stolen from the Virgin Mary in churches around the world.

One month before we meet, he wins a competition and is invited to participate in the International Biennale in Norway with his soft-sculpture project. While he struggles to get the consistency right, his mother sends him an email to let him know about my show with the baby, and he comes to find me.

I ask Lucio if he framed his copy or mine. He asks me what I've been doing all this time. The question decimates me. I lay out a sampler of easy answers, bridges to elsewhere. Then I look him in the eye and manage to make an opportune joke.

He brings out a bottle of wine and makes one last remark about Norway. This leads him into an explanation, his voice thicker now, of his gelatin project. He wants to use it to record whatever movements his hand makes as it travels through the air for fifteen to twenty seconds. Attached to his fingers, the gelatin will accompany the movement and render it solid to a maximum height of three feet. Any higher and the filament gets progressively thinner and could break, causing it to shrink back and deform the figure.

Lucio rests his fingers on the mound. He pulls out five diagonal lines with his arm outstretched and guides them downward in a curve. The figure dissolves.

The sound of a key in the lock is added to the scene. His mother walks in and greets us. She's traded her green gloves for a T-shirt that says *Denmark*. Lucio tells her she's picked the wrong country. His mother explains that she's trying out a system invented by Dag that involves announcing one's mood with T-shirts. *Denmark* is, logically, bad news.

We're constantly together. He makes nervous calculations to avoid my touch, abandoning a comfortable spot on the sofa or bending like a reed (I've never seen a reed) to find his twelve inches of personal space. I tell him I want to sleep with him, to see the expressions that pleasure puts on my face through his. This is not a subject he's willing to discuss. He doesn't do much talking.

We have dinner with Lucio's mother and Dag in the apartment next door. She waves around the half-page spread with the photo of me, the baby, his father, and Lucio. She thinks it's marvelous that the passage of time and my brief incursion into obscurity haven't affected our relationship. According to Dag, the key is a shared ancestor from some distant time and place, completely impossible to verify; he cites Genghis Khan, who fathered two thousand children and whose genetic imprint is currently traceable in more than fifteen million, as a case in point. A pause, forks suspended in the air. Dag throws in a positive remark about my piece and the baby. Lucio's mother sets her jaw and reaches across the table, saying "a shining example" as she tweaks my nose. Lucio is suddenly made of glass, or has been emptied out.

She asks me what the baby's malformation is called. I don't remember. Dag hypothesizes that the presence of two heads on a single body is the result of an unresolved struggle between the DNA of two equally strong ancestral lines, and that with just a movement of his neck, the baby could be either Jekyll or Hyde. The cutting response he gets from Lucio's mother has Dag ending the day in a shirt that says *Chile.*

As a pretext for spending more time with him, I offer to help Lucio solve his gelatin problem. I contend that his soft sculpture runs the risk of becoming the "charming" piece in the Biennale, the sort of interactive object that offers momentary respite and is always surrounded by women with children. Plus, getting the gelatin from boiled cow bones is awkward. I propose working with materials derived from petroleum. The deadline to submit the piece is three weeks away. Like a curtain falling on our search, a chemical engineer tells us that if someone were to find a way to defy gravity using petroleum products, the art world would be the last to know about it.

Lucio lets the gelatin go but insists that the object should be soft, so it conforms, if only partially, to the project he proposed for the Biennale. I tell him that I respect his scruples, but that we should set them aside just this once and start working, together, on a more effective piece.

We have the relics he stole from the Virgin. We should include an account of their theft, to give them an air of impropriety. There's an eighteenth-century rosary with sapphire beads long enough to fit around at least three necks. Lucio remembers the minuscule hands on the Virgin it came from. I remember his mother's gloves. We add the idea of a hand holding the rosary. Lucio still insists on movement. I describe the living hell of a last-minute consultation with an expert in animatronics; anyway, a hand holding a rosary and moving around in the middle of an empty room doesn't justify the expense. But fifty hands do. They should move and be soft. The least expensive movement is vibration. Lucio wants to make fifty child-sized hands out of silicone and run a copper wire through them, send a current through every ten seconds to make them quiver, and hang the whole thing at least five feet in the air. Like the beads of a rosary. A rosary made of praying hands. Dag says a Norwegian audience will hate the obvious symbolism of the piece and argues with Lucio about Norwegianness. An undesired outcome of their conversation is that my mind turns to Argentineanness. I recall the theft of Perón's hands. Evita's body became a relic the day she died; Perón's hands become a relic as a result of their theft. In this new symbolic pun, we have Christian relics obtained by theft and a theft that produces its relic. Lucio draws a circle in the air with his finger. He says that the installation has no theoretical foundation whatsoever, but that no one will be the wiser if we call it *Perón*. Dag likes it because he's been obsessed with Evita since he arrived in Buenos Aires. I suggest taking his opinion into account as a barometer for a hypothetical audience comprised exclusively of Norwegians. For those who don't know about the theft of Perón's hands, I suggest projecting an informational text in white letters at ankle height. It could rotate, making it harder to read. The suggestion, which implies having people bend or fall over as part of the piece, is immediately approved.

We discard the format of the rosary: Lucio finds it pedantic, and I don't think it's justifiable. The Virgin's accoutrements—

no more than three—should be on the floor. The hands should hang in pairs at different heights, with each pair suspended from its own electrical cord; they should move at regular intervals and be real hands, taken from the dead or amputees. The public should be informed of this before entering.

The only legal avenue open to us is to visit the morgue in search of unclaimed hands, with fake paperwork certifying our scientific research. Lucio bribes an older gentleman from the medical school with Dag's money. He gets the money back five minutes later when he steals it out of the gentleman's pocket as they say good-bye. Though I suppose a real theft would have required more effort.

In the morgue, an orderly places the remains on a counter with a drain. There are four loose heads, a fifth one with its mouth open still attached to the torso, and a few arms. There are no legs. The hands have deep creases, small fingers marked with ink, stains like drops of wine. Once removed from the formaldehyde, they will keep for up to four hours: this is how long the installation should last. We obtain the hands of a mother and a rural schoolteacher, illiterate and lettered hands.

Dag is Norwegian, which is uncommon in South America, and has a knack for bribery. In a single week, he manages to sidestep all the legal hurdles put in place to keep Argentinean hands from crossing the ocean to summer in Oslo. In contrast, the paperwork to get my name added to the catalog of the Biennale alongside Lucio's is an object lesson in the incorruptibility of the Norwegian people. At the airport in Oslo, Lucio's mother says we should think of the episode as a contradiction.

Lynda Carter describes the installation's success through a series of incidents unrelated to the piece itself: the story on the local news emphasizing the "reality" of the hands, which boosts the Biennale's attendance by 40 percent; the fainting, anachronistic; the tussle between the event director and our assistant, both remarkably tall women, over a request to extend the show's hours that risked compromising the hands' state of conservation; the Argentinean media's response to the "disrespectful" use of the memory of General Perón; the outcry at our being awarded second prize though we were the crowd favorite. I sense Lucio's involvement in the selection of details.

Two days before the Biennale ends, its organizers decide to combat overcrowding by adding several square feet from our neighbor's exhibition space to our own. This leads to a diplomatic chat with a Swiss artist who's just lost half his space to us. His work is a series of eight counterfeit Van Eycks, painted on canvases from the fifteenth century. They could have generated resplendent profits on the black market, had they not been legalized and devalued by the introduction of a single contemporary element in each. The man in *The Arnolfini Portrait,* for example, is holding a ballpoint pen. In the Ghent altarpiece *The Adoration of the Lamb,* the lamb has Churchill's face. Lucio makes a clever remark about firstworld art and saunters through the space as if he's carrying a parasol, proprietary about controlling his face

At the closing ceremony, Lucio translates "second place" for me in a whisper, his lips grazing my neck as if he were too weary to make it all the way to my ear. To my right, at the same time or maybe a moment earlier, Lucio's mother and Dag's incredulous wail of "second place" washes over the judges and all of Norway. The uproar spreads outward in a circle of heads shaking in disapproval as one.

The Peronists and Silvio Soldán, who has just reminded the media of my prodigious childhood, are waiting for us at the airport back in Buenos Aires. The rational choice would be to pass through without giving a statement and maintain absolute silence until the strategy, a classic, sparks the public's interest. During the month we spend installing the piece in the Palais de Glace, we get legal clearance and a police escort for the hands, courtesy of a judge who followed our experience in Norway with the concern of someone who believes in moral victories. Easy as that.

Lucio launches the Argentinean version of *Perón* by paying two no-name graffiti artists to cover the walls of the Palais de Glace in Peronist slogans denouncing the piece—without consulting me. I find out from the evening news, like the staff of the Palais and the Peronists. Without the slightest glimmer of remorse, Lucio waits for me to ask why he did it. My shoulders slump. I tell him I applaud his antics, but it would have been more daring to take credit for the graffiti as part of the installation.

I'm looking at three photos from the show's opening. In the first, Lucio and I stand alone, hands hanging around us. The Palais is about to open its doors. Lucio points to my bandaged left hand with almost deplorable pride. The corners of his mouth are turned down, his chin juts forward, and his eyelids are stiff at half-mast. My face is frozen in an expression of vindication and pain: the sacrifice is mine.

The second photo is a close-up of me or Lucio posing with the two-headed baby and his father. In the background, nearly in focus, is the man in the tweed suit who will have a fistfight with Lucio in front of the TV crews twenty minutes later, but not before ruining the picture my parents try to take with me by tripping and falling in front of the camera. My father observes his misfortune with a faint smile.

My mother is looking at my ring finger, which hangs with the hands from a wire outside the frame of the image. She wonders if her maternal rights over my body extend to an amputated finger; whether she now has less son to love and protect; whether she actually feels bad about it, considering the success the maneuver has brought me. These questions stamp on her face an expression that is new to her repertory, and it is captured in the picture.

I don't know what part of me is lost with that finger, Lynda, but I am forged in the experience.

# 4

When I say I lost my finger, what I mean is that someone stole it on the last day of the show, an amusing detail that Lucio seems to have forgotten, and which might provide a colorful footnote to your dissertation.

In the period following the Mexican installation of the piece, I'm struck by all the things I can buy at twenty-four, by the studio Lucio and I set up together in Buenos Aires, and by the solicitous speculation of the jealous. The bar for vicarious ambition is apparently set quite low.

Lucio plans. He says it would be a good idea to include dead matter in our next installation. He's too taken with continuity, the excitement of having an artistic program, and the mythos of the Pampas. I insist on avoiding bones and gelatin. Lucio accepts in part. I let myself be taken out to the country in search of a cow that can be "plasticized in the act of grazing."

The incomprehensible language of the farmhands contributes to the expedition's failure. There are thirty cows. Night is falling. Lucio's face is deep in the mud. He's just taken the most clumsy and complicated spill of his life, which has left his leg tangled in a spiral of barbed wire. Laughing uncontrollably, I push his terrible frustration from center stage. This is how I show my love.

The closest thing to science around there is a veterinarian in a half-buttoned lumberjack shirt who asks me to hold Lucio down while he tries to remove the barbed wire. In a thin voice, Lucio declines. He tries to get the wire out himself, but it's stuck deep in the flesh. He believes, I think, that his

humiliation will be less humiliating if he courageously with-
stands the pain that crowns it until we reach the sanatorium
some twenty miles away. I watch him hop a quarter mile across
an open field to reach the car. The veterinarian tells him to lie
down in the back seat and stick his injured leg out the window. To top it all off, it's raining.

The timeworn grounds that separate Temperley Sanatorium's
main gate from its three pavilions provide the last phase
in the martyrdom of Lucio's leg. A man follows us: he has
remarkably long arms, and the fly of his pants is stuck open.
Hunched over, he inspects the problem. He came out from
behind a tree.

The place follows the standard design of hospitals from
the nineteen hundreds—unpleasant at night, confusing—but
despite the darkness and the fact that he's looking down, the
man doesn't make a single false step. I don't look back again,
so I'm spared the sight of his face when he runs out of patience
with his zipper. He follows us to the door of the main pavilion
and then keeps going toward the garden.

Lucio stains the carpeting of the deserted reception area
with the mud from his shoes. We catch a glimpse of the receptionist at the far end of a long hallway. She has her back to us
and seems lost in the contemplation of a nearly perfect circle
of ants on the wall. I ask Lucio not to call to her just yet; I want
to see how long it takes her to snap out of it. The nearly thirty
seconds that she lasts come by regularly with my lack of consideration for Lucio's injured leg.

The receptionist comes trotting toward us.

I hear him squeal like a pig inside one of the rooms. The receptionist offers me a coffee and asks if we're there on purpose,

by accident, or because of some extraordinary circumstance. Whichever I choose, I'll be expected to supply a few details, and details lead to conversations. Not to mention the coffee, which already sets the stage for an exchange of confidences. I reply, "On purpose." Luckily, the wall opposite the reception desk is covered with memorabilia, which allows me to keep my back to her.

I see an official certificate embellished with the face of Eva Perón, an English or Irish coat of arms, a craniometer, a row of ceramic jars, photographs of each of the original medical staff of the sanatorium—the same pointy mustache on every face—and an oil portrait of the owner and founder, Mr. R. Allomby, proudly displaying a burn that disfigures his mouth.

"That friend of yours sure has a set of pipes on him," says the receptionist, passing me the coffee. "Since you don't seem to want to talk to me, maybe you should go keep him company."

I trust I'll be able to find my way to him by just following the screams, but the high ceilings mangle the sound. Every door around the perimeter is closed. There is a tiny sign with an arrow that says *Security*. At the end of the hall, I see a door ajar and the man with the long arms peering in, hunched over as if the most interesting part of Lucio's treatment were happening in the bottom three feet of the room.

My footsteps don't frighten him. As I get closer, I notice his fly is still open. It's Sebastian. His sunglasses have left dents in his temples. He asks, his eyes duller than I remembered, if Lucio is me a hundred pounds lighter, and who I am.

Sebastian's sunglasses are covered in sweat, his pants chafe, it's too bright. His break at the side of the road gives him a good view of the other cyclists riding into the distance. It's the perfect opportunity to disappear from my life. He doesn't feel stifled by me yet, but decisions don't require much of a rationale at nineteen.

That night he meets some guy who takes him to Chile. After three more relationships, he's saved enough money for the classic trip around Latin America. He's invited to a yoga retreat in the shadow of an Incan temple aligned with the solstices, where he's bitten by a snake. The swelling from the venom puts pressure on his eyes, making them even more sensitive to light. By twenty-four, he's back in Buenos Aires as a low-earning night owl.

He doesn't talk about his mother. From his grandfather César he inherits: a collection of photographs and documents from Temperley Sanatorium, a notebook full of minuscule writing and obscene drawings (penises, a bidet, a diminutive vagina on the last page) signed by his great-grandfather, one Doctor Quintana, and more than ten ceramic jars labeled "come-madre," the dark and seemingly ancient contents of which remain enigmatic until he reads the notebook.

He offers the empty jars and the photos to the new owner of the sanatorium, which will now have a history to boast. In exchange, he negotiates a temporary stay in an unused room in Pavilion Three and helps tend the garden.

Sebastian guides me to the reception desk to show me the photos of his forubears. It's a sweet gesture. "This is the original owner of the frogs that left me blind," he says. "He gave them to my great-grandfather, who's this one here. The one on the right was his enemy. They both wanted her."

There she is, straight as a rod and poised to receive an order, in a 1907 advertisement promising a cure for cancer. Clearly, the current owner of the sanatorium would rather have a dubious history than none at all.

Lynda: I'm attaching a reproduction of Doctor Quintana's manuscript. It might complement your study nicely. What follows is what Sebastian told me—it's not a summary, but rather everything he knows about the subject.

Quintana believes a modest existence is enough for her. He often asks her what she does when she's alone, what rituals bind her to the world when he can't see her. Just in case, he removes the bidet from her bathroom before the move and forbids her from working or smoking, though she may have been the first respectable woman to smoke in Argentina. Without this trailblazing gesture or her position as the head nurse, Menéndez is nothing to write home about. There's no information about what form her love for him took.

Quintana quits his post at Temperley Sanatorium one month after the fire, and his colleagues throw him a farewell asado. His senses sharpened by alcohol, he notices that all of them have magnificent scars from the blaze—while he does not. He draws an ephemeral conclusion about the nature of heroism.

At some point, Menéndez finds Quintana's notebook and reads it cover to cover. She says nothing. Shortly thereafter, she gives birth to a freckled baby they name César.

Quintana attempts to blow his brains out in 1932. He locks himself in the bathroom, shouting about what he plans to do. Menéndez asks the cleaning lady to break the lock for her. Nothing more is said of the incident. He retires that year. Sebastian still has a photo of him on his first day as a pensioner: he's hunched over, his hands resting on the counter beside the teller window.

César, a loudmouthed and spoiled child, develops bad skin, a problematic attitude, and a fondness for prostitutes and Mussolini—attributes that turn him into a colorful figure who lives on in family lore in the form of outrageous anecdotes.

Lucio tells Sebastian where to wash his hands, where to sit, what he shouldn't touch; right now, he's handing him a stick of deodorant. It's his (extremely) vulgar way of keeping him at a distance. Sebastian talks about us, about how fat I was, how he fell in love with me right away. Every now and then he breaks through Lucio's perimeter, touching his shoulder or bringing his face in close enough to graze his nose as he calls him by my name, either because of his poor vision or because he doesn't remember me well. He must think we want sex. Lucio's after something much worse: inspiration.

It's a black powder with an irregular texture. Its name in Spanish, *comemadre*, died out with the Patagonian crop eighty years ago, but it lives on in England as *motherseeker* or *mothersicken*. The last remaining plants are held by the English mafia, which uses the larvae to dispose of evidence. This is according to Sebastian. The rest of the information comes from a dead doctor's notes. With water? Just like that? After a whole century? Seeds have stayed dormant longer. It pushes the limits of credibility, but Lucio wears the placid expression of a true believer.

He wants the installation to be a circle of guillotines constructed according to the description in Quintana's notebook, and he wants the larvae to eat something, live. In his verbal incontinence, he even goes so far as to mention video screens. I tell him I find his idea arbitrary and insipid but invite him to keep digging around in my past to see what he finds. I give him permission to use Sebastian, Sebastian's ancestors, the finger I lost, and the two-headed baby from my solo show. He says I can keep the baby: shining the spotlight on an anomaly is a license that can only be taken once—in a rookie piece meant to stir up trouble, like mine. I remind him that the amputated finger did the same. His reply: "We owe that finger almost everything: it's as effective as a fart joke in geography class. Your part in it, though, would've meant more in the nineteenth century, without anesthesia." I ask him what cheap brand of romanticism led him to view pain as a form of artistic honesty.

I see our physical differences blurred by daily use: my head is less round, my lips are fuller, I use different facial muscles to express anger; his face is as smooth as a baby's, and I shave once a week.

Years after Liberace plows into a rhinestone piano and thinks to have his boyfriend undergo surgery to look just like him, but before Orlan wonders what she might gain from going under the knife, the first true monster was made in Buenos Aires, fully aware of itself and of the art world that would watch it grow. "That's what we'll do, because we have the means, and because we were the first to think of it." A point of pride, the mark of our vanity. Some critics (Lynda included) assume the piece can be traced back to the dictatorship, to the mutilation of Evita's body, and—yet again, ad nauseam—to Esteban Echeverría's "The Slaughter Yard."

Confirmed: droplets of water administered to the black powder revive the comemadre. The plant loosely resembles a cactus.

After eight weeks the larvae appear; they reach their maximum density per cubic millimeter in week ten.

We have the idea for a real human leg injected with come-madre larvae dissolving onstage and leaving a black residue that quivers with mouths and legs under the microscope. Lucio wants several legs doing a cripple's can-can, which the public would direct by administering electric shocks. I'm seduced by the can-can and the interactive element, but not by revisiting the mechanization of our last piece. Anyway, I don't want to go through the whole thing with the morgue again. One leg is enough. I propose that we use one attached to a living person.

We need to find someone suggestible and desperate for money who can sit perfectly still on a bicycle (it must be a bicycle) while the larvae eat through his leg below the knee. Common sense dictates that the leg should be sectioned off beforehand so the larvae don't work their way through the whole person.

The surgeon who performs this procedure will also be in charge of erasing any differences between our faces, however minor. We've already gotten good exposure from our names; now we can add a single, unmistakable face. Lucio Lavat thinks the gesture is redundant. I bet my life on its mediatic power.

There aolta which one of us will be the model. He argues, in his favor, that it's easier to remove hair than it is to make some appear where it doesn't naturally grow; as such, I'll need to reduce the size of my lips and earlobes, start taking hormones to control hair growth, and file down a few sections of my skull. "Sounds juvenile," Dag says over the phone. A week later, he's landed our first investors. The fact that someone is willing to finance the project throws us off, as if we'd been betting all along that failure would protect us from our decision.

Lucio has an almost-stolen Beardsley on his résumé, but I have a finger amputated by choice on mine, and we're not talking about irreversible changes. I offer up my body for the surgery. "You'd like to cut me out of the piece," Lucio says.

Dag suggests it would be healthier for both of us to use a third party, imaginary or real, as the model. The imaginary candidates (Bette Davis, Mantegna's Christ, Perón) fall to the wayside for being too referential, and because no surgeon could fashion those faces for us without degrading them. Our model needs to be real. Lucio adds a degree of difficulty by pointing out that it should be the person who gives up a leg in the name of art.

The air of historical significance lends itself to an easy yes. Sebastian looks at the numbered grid we've just drawn on his face. The most challenging sector to reproduce is the nose, which starts out quite narrow but then widens down at the nostrils; for our surgeon, this means filing down bone at the top, filling in the base, and inserting a counterbalance. The best option for getting his square forehead is a titanium implant held in place by the natural tension of the scalp. Lip reductions are in order. Luckily, his jawline is similar to ours. The rest is just a matter of losing weight, learning to slouch at the correct angle, and getting his skin tone right, with the help of a professional makeup artist.

The process takes three months, including time for healing and rest. With each strip of gauze that is removed, a new section of Sebastian's face appears, imprinted on our own. The multiplication of his face leaves him satisfied, relaxed, as if he could finally set his life on the path toward something extraordinary.

In the film record of *Cartesian Doc: Pathos and Method,* we sit on the operating table, watching Sebastian exercise on his stationary bicycle. Sebastian watches the comemadre larvae hollow out his leg from inside on a monitor attached to an electron microscope. His foot remains on the pedal when it detaches from the ankle. We imitate Sebastian's expressions of pain with the one-second delay we've rehearsed.

Because of some problem with the medium, we don't look as identical in the digital video of the piece.

Dag returns to Argentina with Lucio's mother and organizes a dinner for the four of us. At the last minute, he invites Lucio's father. They haven't spoken since the wedding in Norway.

Lucio's father is wearing a flawless gray suit. Dag, in sweatpants, gives him a long hug. He thinks Argentineans give each other bear hugs.

The father starts a conversation about the price per square foot of New York City real estate. We talk about that. Then he tells us that a hotel maid cornered him in an elevator and congratulated him on his three identical sons, then added that she was very sorry about the leg. From this, he deduces that the piece must be quite popular. He congratulates us.

Lucio's mother reminisces out loud about the day she discovered her first husband was missing a testicle. The funniest part, according to her, wasn't its absence, which she never minded, but the fact that she only found out after fifteen years of marriage, thanks to an EMT who'd revived him after a heart attack.

Lucio's father pauses in the middle of chewing a piece of meat, which gives us time to debate the credibility of the story and imagine a sex life based on hang-ups and unhealthy shame. Though Lucio's mother doesn't go into detail on the matter, she does insist she's telling the truth. Dag asks if they ever considered a testicular implant. Lucio's father manages to answer that no, no they didn't, before something lodges itself in his throat. Dag knocks him on the back. Lucio's mother says that of all possible forms discomfort could take, her ex-husband always chooses the most vulgar.

"You'll have to show us, Dad," says Lucio.

Dear Lynda, I can't help you with your idea for the end of the dissertation. What theoretical gain could there possibly be in pointing out the physical changes that come with time? The current photo you request simply isn't possible. I haven't heard from Sebastian since he confided in me that he was going to start cultivating comemadre to sell to the local mafia.

Please let Lucio know that the museum in Copenhagen sent me a dossier of the project involving my jarred hamster, Wright, and my cadaver; if I agree to sell it to them (they call it a "compensated donation"), I get a lifetime pension and can curate the room where I'll be exhibited. Maybe Lucio can arrange something similar with a museum in Oslo.

Barricaded in a closet, the father calls the police. Officials find the two-headed baby lying facedown in the flooded backyard. The still-inarticulate shrieks are coming from the lone posterior mouth. As the days go by, he begins to form complete words and sentences, usurping his brother's voice. An interviewer asks what he thinks about the forced coexistence. Below, the transcript I promised:

*I feel cold and hunger like him, and with him, but it's his body. He's the one who sees and breathes. If there's an itch, he's the one who scratches. I hear his thoughts like a prosthesis over my own, as if someone sewed a foot onto my feet or an eye onto my eye.*

*Our memories, though, are different.*

*If my face pointed toward him, I'd chew through his neck with these teeth. Sooner or later, I'd get to the spine. Neutralize him. Even if I miscalculated, if I bit too deep and he died, I'd still have a few seconds before I expired to take in the world as me, and only me.*

*Buenos Aires, September 2009*

LITERATURE
is not the same thing as
PUBLISHING

Coffee House Press began as a small letterpress operation in 1972 and has grown into an internationally renowned non-profit publisher of literary fiction, essay, poetry, and other work that doesn't fit neatly into genre categories.

Coffee House is both a publisher and an arts organization. Through our *Books in Action* program and publications, we've become interdisciplinary collaborators and incubators for new work and audience experiences. Our vision for the future is one where a publisher is a catalyst and connector.

## FUNDER ACKNOWLEDGMENTS

Coffee House Press is an internationally renowned independent book publisher and arts nonprofit based in Minneapolis, MN; through its literary publications and *Books in Action* program, Coffee House acts as a catalyst and connector—between authors and readers, ideas and resources, creativity and community, inspiration and action.

Coffee House Press books are made possible through the generous support of grants and donations from corporations, state and federal grant programs, family foundations, and the many individuals who believe in the transformational power of literature. This activity is made possible by the voters of Minnesota through a Minnesota State Arts Board Operating Support grant, thanks to the legislative appropriation from the arts and cultural heritage fund. Coffee House also receives major operating support from the Amazon Literary Partnership, the Jerome Foundation, the McKnight Foundation, Target Foundation, and the National Endowment for the Arts (NEA). To find out more about how NEA grants impact individuals and communities, visit www.arts.gov.

Coffee House Press receives additional support from the Elmer L. & Eleanor J. Andersen Foundation; the David & Mary Anderson Family Foundation; Bookmobile; the Buuck Family Foundation; Fredrikson & Byron, P.A.; Dorsey & Whitney LLP; the Fringe Foundation; Kenneth Koch Literary Estate; the Knight Foundation; the Matching Grant Program Fund of the Minneapolis Foundation; Mr. Pancks' Fund in memory of Graham Kimpton; the Schwab Charitable Fund; Schwegman, Lundberg & Woessner, P.A.; the U.S. Bank Foundation; and VSA Minnesota for the Metropolitan Regional Arts Council.

## THE PUBLISHER'S CIRCLE OF COFFEE HOUSE PRESS

Publisher's Circle members make significant contributions to Coffee House Press's annual giving campaign. Understanding that a strong financial base is necessary for the press to meet the challenges and opportunities that arise each year, this group plays a crucial part in the success of Coffee House's mission.

Recent Publisher's Circle members include many anonymous donors, Suzanne Allen, Patricia A. Beithon, the E. Thomas Binger & Rebecca Rand Fund of the Minneapolis Foundation, Andrew Brantingham, Robert & Gail Buuck, Claire Casey, Louise Copeland, Jane Dalrymple-Hollo, Mary Ebert & Paul Stembler, Kaywin Feldman & Jim Lutz, Chris Fischbach & Katie Dublinski, Sally French, Jocelyn Hale & Glenn Miller, the Rehael Fund-Roger Hale/Nor Hall of the Minneapolis Foundation, Randy Hartten & Ron Lotz, Dylan Hicks & Nina Hale, William Hardacker, Randall Heath, Jeffrey Hom, Carl & Heidi Horsch, Amy L. Hubbard & Geoffrey J. Kehoe Fund, Kenneth Kahn & Susan Dicker, Stephen & Isabel Keating, Kenneth Koch Literary Estate, Cinda Kornblum, Jennifer Kwon Dobbs & Stefan Liess, Lambert Family Foundation, Lenfestey Family Foundation, Sarah Lutman & Rob Rudolph, the Carol & Aaron Mack Charitable Fund of the Minneapolis Foundation, George & Olga Mack, Joshua Mack & Ron Warren, Gillian McCain, Malcolm S. McDermid & Katie Windle, Mary & Malcolm McDermid, Sjur Midness & Briar Andresen, Maureen Millea Smith & Daniel Smith, Peter Nelson & Jennifer Swenson, Enrique & Jennifer Olivarez, Alan Polsky, Marc Porter & James Hennessy, Robin Preble, Alexis Scott, Ruth Stricker Dayton, Jeffrey Sugerman & Sarah Schultz, Nan G. & Stephen C. Swid, Kenneth Thorp in memory of Allan Kornblum & Rochelle Ratner, Patricia Tilton, Joanne Von Blon, Stu Wilson & Melissa Barker, Warren D. Woessner & Iris C. Freeman, Margaret Wurtele, and Wayne P. Zink & Christopher Schout.

For more information about the Publisher's Circle and other ways to support Coffee House Press books, authors, and activities, please visit www.coffeehousepress.org/support or contact us at info@coffeehousepress.org.

# RECENT LATIN AMERICAN TRANSLATIONS
## FROM COFFEE HOUSE PRESS

*After the Winter*
Guadalupe Nettel
Translated by Rosalind Harvey

*Among Strange Victims*
Daniel Saldaña París
Translated by Christina MacSweeney

*Camanchaca*
Diego Zuñíga
Translated by Megan McDowell

*Empty Set*
Verónica Gerber Bicecci
Translated by Christina MacSweeney

*Faces in the Crowd*
Valeria Luiselli
Translated by Christina MacSweeney

*The Story of My Teeth*
Valeria Luiselli
Translated by Christina MacSweeney

ROQUE LARRAQUY is an Argentinean writer, screenwriter, professor of narrative and audiovisual design, and author of two books, *La comemadre* and *Informe sobre ectoplasma animal.* In 2016, he was named the director of Argentina's first degree-granting program in creative writing, housed at the Universidad Nacional de las Artes, a public institution. *Comemadre* is his first book published in English.

HEATHER CLEARY's translations include Sergio Chejfec's *The Planets* and *The Dark,* both nominated for national awards, and a selection of Oliverio Girondo's poetry. She is a founding member of the Cedilla & Co. translation collective and a founding editor of the digital, bilingual *Buenos Aires Review,* has served as a judge for the BTBA, and teaches at Sarah Lawrence College.

*Comemadre* was designed by
Bookmobile Design & Digital Publisher Services.
Text is set in Minion Pro.